THE THREE VESTS II
MUSICULAR

ROBERT BOWMAN

Hey, stop!

**Don't even think about reading this sequel
unless you've read the first book of the
series, *The New Brilliants*.**

ARE YOU READY?

ISBN 13: 978-0-9713530-5-3
ISBN 10: 0-9713530-5-0

You are reading the third printing.

Printed in the United States.

DEDICATION

For the students I've had the privilege to teach.
You are amazing!

SUMMARY OF BOOK I:
THE NEW BRILLIANTS

While exploring a familiar cave, three friends, Samantha, George, and Juan discover a hidden Chest in one of the caverns. Reluctantly, they open it only to find that they are given mysterious Gifts. Samantha, with the Gift of Knowledge, Juan, the Gift of Invisibility, and George, with the ability to fly.

The three characters attempt to learn these Gifts, for each time their powers come to them, a Vest of Light appears over their chests. Yet, only those with Gifts are able to see the Vests of Light.

Not knowing why they have been given these powers, the three "Brilliants," what those with Vests of Light are called, must try to understand how they will use the powers without drawing attention to themselves.

They quickly realize they are not the only ones with special abilities. There are other Brilliants as well, along with the dangerous "Dark Vests." The Dark Vests use their powers to destroy the Brilliants and serve their leader, Xylo.

In the end, the new Brilliants are saved from death by the Robe, an older man with many powers, who, instead of a Vest of Light, wears a Robe of Light. The New Brilliants have many questions that the Robe does not give complete answers to, and the Brilliants are left feeling as though they know very little about the Dark Vests or the new world they've become a part of.

Prologue

"The time is now. How long I have waited for this. Finally — finally we have what we need to defeat the Brilliants. We have a Musicular."

THE LAXINTOTH
August 15

Malavax had not anticipated the rain. Hunting a Laxintoth was tough enough, but the pounding rain, coupled with the darkness, was making it much more difficult. She hadn't figured on a downpour like this in mid-August, but then again she didn't know Sonora, Mexico very well. She didn't know that thunderstorms were quite frequent during the summer, especially at night.

Standing under a mesquite tree, she attached the glowing, thick Belt around her waist. Immediately, it began to pulsate with bright, white light and her eyes turned from dark brown to transparent. She could see clearly now as though it were daytime, even in the black of night. She was out in the desert, and besides a few scattered farms, the only other sign of civilization was the small *ciudad* of Magdalena nearly thirty miles away.

She moved out from under the tree and zipped the heavy windbreaker around her tightly. The night was warm — Malavax liked the heat, but it was the suffering rain that drove her crazy. Thunder echoed in the distance, followed by an explosion of lightning that lit up the cloud-filled sky in brief intervals.

She had been following the trail for nearly an hour in the pouring rain and wondered if Ivory really knew what she was talking about this time. True, she had led Malavax to the first three Laxinti, but this fourth Laxintoth had been elusive, much more so than the others Malavax had captured.

Another lightning burst and a roll of thunder far away took her attention off the trail, toward where the sound had come from. She stared at the sky, waiting for the next shot of lightning when something to her right caught her attention. She turned, and hovering behind another tall mesquite tree, its wings beating gently, was the unmistakable glow of a Laxintoth.

Malavax froze. She watched as it moved out from behind the branches and descended to the ground, its back turned to her. She couldn't actually see it, but she knew that the Laxintoth was placing a Chest of Light on the ground. She raised both arms slowly until they were stretched in front of her and then concentrated. Two rays of dark light shot out of her fingertips, merged into one beam, and struck the Laxintoth in its back. Part of the Spirit's wing broke, and it let out a shrill cry of pain. That's when Malavax knew this particular Laxintoth was female.

She charged through the muddy ground toward the Spirit as it fell and rolled over onto its back. She had to get there before it was able to get up . . . too late.

The Laxintoth had gotten to her feet.

Malavax stopped; she knew what was coming next. But was she fast enough?

The Laxintoth raised her hand slightly, and a beam of light sped toward Malavax. She tried to duck, but the light caught in her neck and propelled her backwards twenty feet. She hit the ground hard but was able to stagger to her feet, trying to ignore the throbbing pain in her throat.

The Laxintoth attempted to jump into the air, but her left wing was too damaged, and even though she moved it back and forth, it was no use in helping her become airborne. Malavax stepped up and fired a blast of black light from her hands.

It missed high.

The Laxintoth refocused her attention to Malavax. A bright light shot out from her outstretched hand, and Malavax leaned far enough to the left so that the rocket of white shot past her shoulder without hitting her. Another couple of hits from the Laxintoth, though, and Malavax would lose her.

Taking aim with her hands, Malavax shot another dark beam at the Spirit, and this time it didn't miss high. The beam hit the Laxintoth square in the abdomen. The Spirit doubled over in pain as Malavax fired another beam into her, forcing her to her knees.

Malavax moved slowly forward.

"Four," she said, breathing deeply.

The Laxintoth, still on her knees, looked up at the approaching Dark Vest.

"You will not get all of us."

Malavax approached carefully until she was standing next to the female Laxintoth. "I've gotten four, haven't I?"

"Why do you hunt us?"

Being so close, it was the first time Malavax had taken time to examine the glowing Spirit. This Laxintoth was beautiful. Long, flowing, auburn hair, all one length to her lower back, hung in lazy curls. Her face, just like the other Laxinti, was without blemish, smooth with a deep olive tone. Her face was somehow pure, somehow innocent. Even though her eyes were golden, she wore the same look the others had . . . compassion and love. Traits Malavax loathed.

"I hunt you because it is what Xylo asks of me," Malavax said darkly.

The Laxintoth's golden, semitransparent wings lay motionless, folded against her back.

"You will join the others," Malavax continued. "Soon, we will have captured all of your kind, and then we shall have total control over the Chests and the Gifts."

"The Robe will never allow that to happen for it is written that . . . "

"Silence!" Malavax shouted, enraged. "All of you Laxinti say the same thing. *It is written that the Robe* . . . as far as I'm concerned, that Book you refer to is nothing but idiotic ideas and thoughts written down for the weak-minded to believe. The Dark Vests are stronger, and we will rule soon."

The Laxintoth stared into Malavax's transparent eyes as a

flash of lightning illuminated the sky.

"What's your name?" the Laxintoth spoke.

"You know my name, Spirit. It is Malavax."

"No, what was your name before you changed it?" the Spirit asked compassionately.

Malavax paused, and for the first time in a very long time, spoke her real name.

"Katherine."

"Why have you allowed her to die?" the Laxintoth asked, her golden eyes widening. "Why have you let Katherine Elizabeth Day be consumed by the power of the Dark Vest?"

Again, Malavax paused. Something inside her was aching now, longing to be expressed. She had not heard her real name, Katherine Elizabeth Day, spoken for years. Just hearing it brought back painful images of a past she did not want to remember. As far as she was concerned, Katherine Elizabeth Day died the day she found a Chest of Light and heard the words, "To you, the Gift of Energy."

Malavax stepped back and raised her hand, pointing her fingers at the winged being. "Don't try that with me, Laxintoth. I am strong minded, and you will not bring me back like you did with Aaron."

The Laxintoth was silent but continued staring at Malavax with the same compassionate look. Malavax brought her left arm up so that she could see more clearly the watch that was wrapped around her wrist. The digital time vanished and was replaced with a white haze that remained in the screen for some time before thinning out. When it did, Malavax was staring at the old man, Fingust.

"I have captured the fourth," she said smugly.

"Who's there? I can't see; it's all black," the old man said in a slight panic.

Malavax wiped the watch with her fingers and put it close to her face. She could see Fingust perfectly, thanks to the glowing

Belt around her waist.

"Relax, old man. It's Malavax. Inform Melt that I have captured the fourth one. I need Thry to come and pick us up."

"Right away, Malavax," Fingust slurred. "Thry is here in the Triangle. It shouldn't be long before she gets to you."

"Fine," Malavax said, pushing the only button on the watch as Fingust dissolved into a white mist, only to be replaced by the digital time again.

"You have the Belt of Sight," the Laxintoth said, slumping to the ground and rolling onto her back.

"That's right."

"Let me see it," the Laxintoth said, now in a whisper.

The massive downpour had finally stopped and only a few trace drops fell from the night sky. Malavax unzipped her coat, and pulsating in brilliant gold was the Belt of Sight.

"You do not deserve to wear that. The Belt is how you've been finding us."

"Very good," Malavax said wryly, wiping her long, wet bangs out of her face. "You'll have something to talk about with the others once Thry arrives."

Malavax moved past the wounded Laxintoth and knelt down beside the old Chest. It looked exactly like the others she had taken — wood and metal, old and well used. It was the fourth one of its kind that she alone had captured.

"What's the Gift?" she asked, turning her head toward the winged being.

"Why would I tell you that?" the Laxintoth whispered. "Open it and find out."

"I'm not stupid, Laxintoth. If I open it, the Chest will give out its power and then disappear. And everyone knows that you can possess only one power from a Chest of Light."

"I wouldn't be so sure," the Laxintoth said quietly. "There are many things about the Brilliants that you do not know, Katherine."

"Don't call me that. My name is Malavax," the Dark Vest said, staring at the Chest and then back at the Spirit. "It would be useless for me to open this Chest. Why don't you just tell me what the power is inside?"

"I will not."

"You realize I could destroy you here and now if I wanted? If Xylo wished it, you'd be obliterated," Malavax spat. "Don't tell me. I don't care, Laxintoth. I will know soon enough."

THE GIFT OF SPEED
August 20

The trail to Union Creek Falls hadn't been traveled much this summer; that was obvious. Large pine branches and smaller tamaracks were cluttering the narrow route, as well as a host of wildflowers that Ethan didn't know the name of but appreciated. Most of them were a rich, deep green and a few were actually blooming, sending shoots of yellow and purple combinations into the air.

Ethan stopped to admire them for a moment. He had been to Union Creek more times that he could keep track of, but this was the first time this summer he had ventured to one of his favorite spots, which was surprising. Usually in mid-August, he'd gone up the trail to the falls so many times that it was practically blazed, but this summer had been different.

Maybe it was the fact that he had played an extended baseball season . . . maybe he was just getting older, he thought. Maybe Union Creek and hiking in the wilderness was something he was growing out of. He had turned fourteen the week before. The day had been like any other, and when his mom and dad asked him the same question they always did on his birthday: Do you feel any older, son? he replied with the same response he did every year: Not really.

What did feeling older mean, anyhow? When does one feel older? He figured he'd feel older when he got gray hair or when he got arthritis like his grandmother, but not at thirteen. His actual birthday was just like any other day, except that he happened to have been born on that day, and besides the portable music player and new video game he got, the day had been uneventful, except when Henry Jefferson got a lollypop jammed up his nose when he fell off the jungle gym in Ethan's backyard.

Ethan didn't recall exactly how it all happened, it had taken place so fast. One moment he was going to the cooler to get a Pepsi, and the next he heard this ear-splitting scream. Ethan wheeled around, and there was Henry on the ground, a Dum-Dum sucker jammed into his left nostril.

"What happened?" Ethan remembered asking.

Henry lay completely still, as though the small lollypop was dynamite, and one false move would cause him to spontaneously explode.

"What happened?" Ethan asked again, coming over and kneeling down.

"I don't know," Henry answered in a nasally whisper. "I was climbing to the top pole and lost my balance. I flipped and the sucker must've come out of my mouth!"

"And got jammed in your nose?" Ethan said as straight-faced as he could, which wasn't very straight-faced. His friend looked ridiculous. The only thought racing through Ethan's head was 'thank God it wasn't a Tootsie Pop.'

"Don't laugh." Henry glared. "It hurts."

"I'm not laughing," Ethan said, trying to turn his cheeks down enough to pass for serious. The sucker was jammed further than Ethan thought as he examined Henry's left nostril like a doctor looking over an important x-ray.

"Are you going to help me?" Henry asked, slowly reaching up to his nose and touching the bulging nostril gently.

"Just pull it out."

"No way. It's killin' me!"

"You have to get it out of there."

"But what if it rips my nose open. . . . "

"You jammed it in there without any problem, didn't you?"

"Yeah, but it's stuck now. Maybe I need to go in and have surgery," Henry suggested seriously, still touching his nose. Ethan thought the situation wasn't as grave as Henry was thinking.

Problem: Lollypop stuck in left nostril.

Solution: Pull it out.

"Here, I'll do it," Ethan suggested, grabbing the end of the sucker stick.

"No, don't touch it!" Henry wailed. He was looking even more ridiculous now, sitting up with a lollypop jammed into his nose. How appropriate that Henry, one of the nicest but dumbest of Ethan's friends, had managed to lodge a piece of candy aptly named Dum-Dum.

"It's not a big deal. Just take it out," Ethan announced calmly.

Henry hesitated and looked at his friend apprehensively. "Maybe we can just crush it up in small pieces and then I'll blow it out."

"What? How are you going to crush it up?"

"Get a rock," Henry said, his stupidity rising another notch.

"Henry, JUST PULL IT OUT!"

"Ethan, what are you doing?"

Ethan turned his head and looked back at his mother as she walked out the sliding glass door toward them.

"What are you guys doing?"

"Nothin'. Henry got a sucker stuck in his nose."

Ethan's mother stopped in her tracks like she'd hit an invisible wall. She shook her head, not having completely comprehended what her son had said. "What?"

"Henry fell off the pole, and the sucker got stuck in his nose," Ethan said plainly as if this were a common occurrence.

Mrs. Franklin looked bewildered. "He got a what — stuck where?"

"I got a Dum-Dum stuck in my nostril," Henry stood up and announced, now almost proud of the feat.

"What were you doing?"

"I was climbing up and I flipped off. Somehow, the sucker got stuck."

Mrs. Franklin burst into laughter. It wasn't intended to be a mean, make-fun-of-you type of laugh. It was more like a snicker, and considering the scene, it was a wonder she'd controlled herself that well. It wasn't often that you saw a thirteen-year-old boy lodge a lollypop in his nostril.

Henry stood in front of her now, and Mrs. Franklin straightened up, attempting to look concerned.

"I think it might be really stuck up there. Oh man, I might need surgery."

Mrs. Franklin moved so fast that Henry really didn't feel her grip the sucker stick, nor pull it out of his nose. It was obvious Mrs. Franklin had pulled out a loose tooth a time or two.

"I'll throw this away," she said, shaking her head and turning back to go inside the house.

Henry was fine after that. He hadn't climbed the pole since, and Ethan figured he'd learned his lesson. Ethan smiled, the images taking him away from the trail and the day, but it didn't last long as a golden mass of a dog lumbered through the wildflowers Ethan had been appreciating.

"Taco, get out of the flowers!" Ethan scolded.

The golden dog stopped and raised her ears as if to say: Why? The animal turned her attention to the flowers and opened her mouth, attacking them as if they were an important food source.

"Stupid dog," Ethan said, almost to himself as a reminder that not only did he have Henry, his rather unintelligent friend, but he had a sometimes unin-telligent dog to go with him. "You don't eat flowers."

But Ethan knew this was no use. Taco ate everything, and the fact that she was munching down wild flowers didn't surprise him. He'd had the dog for almost five years, and even when they had gotten her as a six-month-old pup, she had a desire to eat everything and anything. As soon as they had gotten in the car on that first car ride, the dog started on the passenger seatbelt, gnawing it into shreds within a few minutes. So the fact that she was consuming flowers didn't surprise Ethan much. About the only thing he hadn't seen her eat were apples. Besides that, whatever you put in front of her, she ate.

"Get out!" Ethan said firmly.

This time the dog listened and tucked her head down, meandering back to the trail. Ethan followed her, pushing the branches of pine and tamarack out of his way.

Very few people knew of the trail to Union Creek Falls. Ethan loved hiking to it, watching the water pour off the sharp rocks and plummet down into the light blue pool of water. The hike itself was a steep incline and after about a mile, broke off to the left. If you stayed on the main trail, it led away from the falls and looped around to the east, but by taking the fork left, you crisscrossed through a lush green forest of thin birch until finally descending upon the base of the falls.

Ethan took his time along the trail. The outdoors was home to him, and getting away from his younger brothers was time he cherished. Being the oldest had advantages; but it also had disadvantages, and one of them wasn't having a lot of time for yourself, and the dreaded five-word sentence: Take your brothers with you.

But on this particular Saturday, his mom had let him take Taco and go without his brothers, and Ethan loved it. The forest was calm, and the only sounds were those coming from the roaring falls. He broke off to the left and began his descent, winding back and forth in a zigzagged course toward the water. As he rounded a curve, he stopped abruptly and smiled. He hadn't been here in so long he had forgotten about it, but Taco hadn't, that was obvious.

Suspended four feet in the air, the pure golden Lab hung by her mouth, her jaws wrapped around a thick tamarack branch, hanging there like a statue. Ethan shook his head and laughed aloud.

Taco was a unique dog, for sure. There were times when Ethan thought that Taco acted more like a human than an animal, and seeing her hanging by a branch reminded him that he didn't know too many dogs who climbed trees or hung from branches.

The first time he had hiked to Union Creek, Taco couldn't have been more than a year old. He had thrown some dog biscuits in his pocket, and the entire hike she had run around him, playing dead, sitting, barking, and attempting to do anything for a treat. But when Ethan had turned the corner that first time and saw her hanging by her jaws, he figured THAT trick was worth a biscuit or two, and ever since, whenever the two of them hiked to Union Creek, the dog performed the feat.

Ethan pulled a chewy biscuit out of the narrow pocket of his shorts and held it in his hand. Taco still hung on the branch but moved her eyes to the side when he had pulled out the treat.

"Ready?" Ethan asked.

Taco dropped.

He threw the biscuit in the air down the trail, and Taco gave chase. He watched her as she sprinted down and leaped into the air, catching the treat with ease. She nearly swallowed it whole, and then looked up at him. If Ethan didn't know better, he could've sworn the dog smiled. He took another treat out of his pocket and threw it to her. As he walked past, he whispered, "That's all for now."

She seemed to agree and raced past him like she was the scout on an important mission, making sure her master was safe from the wilds of the forest. In another few minutes, Ethan was standing at the base of one of the most beautiful falls in the state of Washington.

The water raged over the granite cliffs and spilled into the inviting blue water before snaking its way into the creek bed on the way to a bigger stream. The day was hot, and he had hoped the sun would stay out from behind the clouds so that when he got to the falls, he could indulge himself.

The pool was a deep, wide hole, perfect for swimming. The only disadvantage was that the water was a glacial stream, and it was COLD. But Ethan had worked up a sweat, and the ninety-degree heat was pounding down, the sun was still high, and the pool of water looked that much more inviting.

He pulled his shirt off and sat down on the sandy shore. He was a tall, skinny teenager, and like his dad at that age, was battling acne on his forehead and back. Usually he was rather self-conscious about taking his shirt off when others were around, but he was alone in the wilderness, and there was no fear of ridicule or disgusted looks and nasty whisperings.

Taco knew the procedure and charged into the pool of water, paddling around, taking large gulps of the fresh liquid. Ethan removed his socks and jumped in. The initial shock of cold took his breath away. Even though he was hot, those first few seconds were always difficult. Taco never seemed to have a problem with the temperature, but Ethan did. It would take a while before his body would acclimate itself to the frigid water.

He breaststroked his way across the pool, staying away from the actual falls. He'd gotten too close one time and the force of the falling water nearly drowned him. He was content to swim in the deeper portion anyhow and held his breath before going under. He popped back up almost immediately, and there was Taco, not a foot away from his face.

"Go away, Taco," he scolded and swam toward the other side, but Taco was chasing him, diligently paddling through the wavy water toward her master. Ethan dove down again, this time deeper, and turned his body so that he could see the blurry outline of his dog trudging along the surface. He waited a few seconds, and then popped up behind her.

"Taco," he shouted, spitting water from his mouth. The dog turned her head and immediately began the process of turning her body back through the choppy water, but Ethan didn't give her the chance. He reached out and grabbed her tail, pulling her toward him.

"Gotcha, girl."

The dog barked, half of the sound muffled by the water that had poured into her mouth. Ethan let her tail go and swam toward the bank until it was shallow enough to stand on the sandy bottom. The water was refreshing, but he knew that staying in for more than a few minutes meant a headache. He had learned from previous visits that a long swim wasn't worth a splitting head.

He walked forward to the beach and lay down on the hot sand. He closed his eyes and felt the warmth of the sun beam down on his face, soaking up the rays as if he were a sponge. Taco emerged from the water and shook herself off in a motion that resembled a washing machine spin cycle.

"Don't do it," Ethan warned, his eyes still closed.

Taco, in some strange way, seemed to understand him, and popped her ears high into the air, tilting her head curiously.

"Don't even think about it, dog. I'm comfortable."

She took a few steps toward him in the sand.

"No, Taco. I don't need that nasty tongue licking me all over the place."

Ethan knew what Taco wanted to do. She did it every time after swimming. As soon as he laid down to get warm, it was the Taco licking fest, and the thought of having his dog's rough, slobbering tongue on his face didn't exactly appeal to him. But it didn't matter. She always attacked, and at any moment he anticipated that he would feel the rough texture of her tongue slapping across his cheeks. To his surprise, it was quiet. The only sound was the roar of the falls. Ethan assumed she'd actually listened this time, but then came her bark, and his hopeful wish of a little peace and quiet was dashed.

"Shut up."

She barked again.

"Shut up!" Ethan said louder. "I wanna rest!"

Taco barked again, and this time it was more intense. Ethan knew his dog well, and the kind of bark he was hearing was a warning.

He opened his eyes and sat up abruptly. Taco was barking aggressively, her ears pinned back, and staring at what looked like an old Chest, like a treasure Chest twenty feet to his right. Ethan stared at it, and for a moment thought that he was seeing things. How could a Chest just suddenly appear from nowhere. He stood up and moved toward it.

"Quiet, girl," he said, rubbing the top of Taco's head before kneeling down beside the large, battered, and weather-beaten Chest. There were three latches on the front: a large one in the center and two smaller ones on the sides.

Taco finally quieted down as Ethan looked around the area, up the trail, and around the base of the falls. How could a Chest like this just end up here? Could someone have brought it down while he'd been swimming?

Impossible. He would've noticed; he hadn't been in the water that long. There wasn't anyone around.

"Where'd this come from?" he whispered to Taco.

She barked as though she was telling him.

"I wish you could talk."

Ethan brought his attention back to the Chest. It was obviously old, with nicks and gashes littering the sides and the top. It was made of wood and well crafted. The edges were smooth and angled, and it was apparent that whoever had built it had taken their time. It was large and looked heavy. Could someone have carried it all the way down here, just to leave it?

His curiosity was bubbling. What was inside the Chest? Would it be right if he opened it? It wasn't his. But maybe the inside would give him some sort of answer as to where it had come from or what it was doing here.

He looked around yet again and then slid his hand toward the center latch. It snapped open without even the slightest touch. Ethan pulled his hand back quickly. He moved his hand to the left, over the clasp, and it, too, snapped open.

"What the . . ."

He paused and then moved his hand over the right-hand latch. It clicked up immediately.

Taco began barking wildly.

Ethan pulled his hand away.

"What? It's just a chest."

She growled angrily.

"Quiet, Taco. Let's see what's inside."

Slowly, he put his hands on the outside edge of the lid and lifted it up.

Taco went silent.

The inside of the Chest was lined with a thick, white linen cloth, and as Ethan looked inside, the first thought that came into his mind was that it was incredibly clean for looking so old. The inside looked new. At the bottom of it was a round, ruler-sized rod. It was light blue and very smooth.

The scene was becoming odder. First, a mysterious Chest appears out of nowhere. The inside of it is impressively clean, and now a very plain looking object lay at the bottom. He reached down and wrapped his fingers around the rod. An energy surged through his hand and almost instantaneously the rod began to glow with an intense bluish hue. Ethan dropped it and watched as the glow faded back to its original light blue. He looked at Taco. Taco stared back.

Both of them were silent.

Ethan looked around again.

Something compelled him to reach in and pick up the rod again. This time he took it out of the Chest and examined it carefully, holding it up toward the sky. It was glowing brightly, and the rich blue that emanated from it was incredible. Ethan had seen blue before, but not like this. He'd never seen a blue light so intense, so rich. It was as though it was alive, and his right hand that held it up was tingling.

He was captured by it, which explained why he didn't notice the white smoke that began to filter out of the Chest. When he finally did notice it, the thick fog had wrapped around him. Taco began barking frantically, and before Ethan had time to tell her to quiet down, a bright light shot through the whiteness and struck him in his upper body.

"To you, the Gift of Speed," a loud voice thundered. Ethan dropped the rod and stared as the light wrapped around his chest and began to sparkle brightly. Within a few moments, the light linked together in a pattern and the outline of a Vest made completely of light wrapped around his upper body. The smoke was abruptly sucked back into the Chest and in a brilliant explosion of light, disappeared.

Ethan was frozen, staring at the powdery, beige sand of the small beach, having just seen an old treasure Chest explode into thin air.

What just happened? He looked down at his bare chest and stared in awe. Sparkles of light came from the Vest, and it reminded him of the way stars pulsate in the night sky. He put his hand to his chest to feel for the light, but his fingers passed through the Vest as though it wasn't there. He turned to look at Taco and couldn't believe what he saw. Wrapped around the dog's body was a blanket of light that shimmered exactly like his Vest. The light danced and bounced back and forth on the blanket like possessed jumping beans.

Taco seemed to be uninterested in her new attire. In fact, Ethan doubted that Taco even knew about the light that encompassed her body. She was more interested in finding the nearest small bush, and he watched her as she went into the thick brush to his left.

Ethan's eyes wandered back to the sand, and there, next to

where the Chest had been, laid the light blue rod. He reached down and picked it up. As soon as his fingers wrapped around it, it glowed and glistened just as it had before.

What was it? Was this some kind of strange dream?

Perhaps it was the blur that caught his attention first or maybe it was Taco's strange bark that seemed to start close and end far away. Regardless, Ethan's day was becoming more bizarre by the moment because, unless he had lost his mind, he had just seen his dog run back up the trail so fast she was a blur of golden hair. When she stopped, she somehow had managed to travel to the top of the knoll in a matter of seconds, when it should've taken much longer.

Could that have been possible? The dog running so fast that she became a blur?

"Taco . . . come here, girl," Ethan called. "Come on, girl. Come 'ere."

He clapped his hands together, studying her carefully. She took a couple of steps and then bam! She turned into a shadow of light, and the next thing he knew she was at his feet panting.

"Sit. Sit down."

She obeyed.

"What is that?" he marveled, putting his hand through the blanket of light that wrapped around her body before turning his attention to his own Vest of Light. The voice said, "The Gift of Speed."

Could he possibly go that fast, too?

Ethan looked at the trail and took off.

What happened next was incredible! The ground, the trees — everything became a mix of color and shadow as he made his way up the trail at super speed. Strangely, he was in complete control of his movements. It felt like he was merely running, but running at an inhuman speed and without effort. Ethan stopped at the top of the knoll, just as Taco had done, and stared down at his Vest. He had some sort of super power. Just as the Chest had said, he had the Gift of Speed.

He turned and watched Taco run toward him, her mouth open with that nasty pink tongue flailing out the left side, but now she was running normally. The blanket of light that had wrapped around her had disappeared. So much for Super Taco!

Ethan felt a chill go down his spine — that kind of chill you get when you feel that things just aren't right, when everything is a mystery, a very odd and scary mystery.

First, an old Chest appears out of nowhere, then the glowing rod and white smoke, not to mention the blinding light and loud voice that shouted: "To you, the Gift of Speed." Everything that was happening felt incredibly real, and Ethan shuddered at the thought that this actually could be the biggest reality sandwich he'd ever taken a bite of.

THE DARK TRIANGLE
September 17 - 12:00 p.m.

The cavern was a maze of corridors and small rooms. How big and long the actual grotto was no one really knew, but it was massive and the perfect center of operations for the Dark Vests.

It was underground on a remote island within the Bermuda Triangle, or Dark Triangle as Xylo referred to it. Hardly anyone in the world knew it existed, and it was impossible to see without having a Vest. That special attribute had been the work of Xylo, and ever since the Dark Vests had been using the lair for their headquarters, not once had it ever been discovered by those who don't possess a Gift.

The largest cavern within the labyrinth of rock was a warehouse-sized, arena-like room. It was always wet from the condensation from the underground river that flowed through the cave, and no matter where you went, you were wet.

How long Melt had been waiting for Xylo he didn't know, but judging by the fact that his thick hair was now completely drenched, he figured close to an hour. The other Dark Vests waiting in the room were growing impatient as well, but none of them dared to say anything. It had been almost five years since Xylo's patience had been tested by Jameson. Jameson had made the mistake of reminding Xylo that there was important work to be done and that time was of the essence. Those turned out to be his last words as Xylo disembodied him on the spot in a matter of seconds.

Melt remembered that day well, even though it had happened years ago. In fact, his memory was full of similar images of his leader, and this was something that gave Melt power. He had served Xylo since becoming a Dark Vest nearly twenty years ago, and at age forty, Melt was one of the most powerful Dark

Vests there were. This was because Xylo trusted him, which was a feat of sorts since Xylo didn't trust anyone; at least that was the consensus among most of the Dark Vests.

"What is the report?" Xylo shouted, emerging from one of the connecting corridors and into the large arena. Melt and the rest of the Dark Vests stood at sudden attention, and what little whispering there was abruptly stopped.

"Everything is proceeding as you ordered, sir," Melt said stoutly.

Xylo approached and laughed . . . a hideous, deep laugh that could only come from someone so evil and vile, even the laugh spewed out invisible poison. And as if the laugh wasn't bad enough, his appearance was worse. His black hair was thinning, and mixed in with the stringy mop were shades of gray and white. The hair stood spiked about two inches high and grew in nearly every direction . . . out the left, to the right, and pressed down over his forehead.

His face was pale and gaunt. His cheeks were sucked in as though he was puckering up to give some disgusting kiss. His lips were a thin layer of pink that barely hid the few black teeth he still had left. Strangely, he had no facial hair, only faded scars that littered his jaw like a bad treasure map.

His fashion was just as bad — a plain, hooded black robe hung down to his feet. He floated when he moved, compliments of the sparkling black robe that always shimmered with a black, shiny luminescence. His robe crackled and sparkled like it was alive with electricity, and many of his followers believed that simply by touching the garment you'd die instantly or contract some terrible disease that would lead to your slow and painful death.

Xylo was almost seven feet tall and very thin. The robe that clothed his body was said to cover the skeleton of a figure, not a man, although none of the Dark Vests had ever seen Xylo in anything but his black robe.

"My brothers and sisters. . . ." He floated past Melt and higher into the air so that all the Dark Vests could see him clearly.

Lined up, single-file, were his followers, his devoted minion. Out of the hundred or so Dark Vests, only about half were present. The others were off on other assignments and missions.

It was a wonder anyone could follow all the goings-on in the Dark Triangle. If it wasn't for Fingust, the ancient coordinator, just about everyone would be without purpose and this would cause Xylo's quick temper to boil over — something everyone wanted to avoid.

"As you know, we have worked for almost a year now on finding a way into the Lighthouse, but it is nearly impossible for us to gain entrance for two reasons. One, only Brilliants are able to transport in, which means, of course, that Thry's power is useless in getting us in. And two, the Bracelets we've captured from the Brilliants don't work unless you are a true Brilliant. The only way in is through a bridge, but in order to complete the bridge, I need a Musicular.

"If I could find a Musicular and establish the bridge, we could enter undetected. Our priority would be finding the Book of Light that resides in the Library as well as taking control of everything the Brilliants have. However, until a Musicular emerges from the Brilliants, we must continue to try and find other ways into their headquarters. Does anyone . . ."

Xylo stopped in mid-sentence and stared down to his right. Stepping forward and turning to address him was a young man of fifteen. Xylo knew exactly who he was, as did everyone else in the cavern. His name was Austin Bennis, nicknamed the Plant Talker because his Gift was the ability to control plant life. Xylo glared at the boy with a look of resentment.

"I'm tired of looking, Xylo. I didn't pledge my allegiance to you just so I could spend every minute trying to find some stupid Book that is . . ."

Melt knew this would happen if the boy interrupted. Anyone who had spent time at Xylo's pep talks knew one simple rule: Never interrupt him. But the boy was pretentious, and Melt had warned him months ago to stay in line and keep his mouth shut. During the next thirty seconds, everyone watched him choke to death.

"Is there anyone else that wishes to speak while I am speaking?" Xylo thundered in rage, as the boy's body lay motionless on the floor.

A very eerie silence followed.

"All of you know your responsibilities, and I want them carried out. By year's end, I want that Book of Light in my hands. You should hope for your sakes that you find a way into the Lighthouse."

Xylo, in a flash of black light, disappeared and with him, Melt. When the two rematerialized, Melt was staring at the Liqwall, a wall he had seen many times before.

"It is a pity I can only transport within the Triangle. Relying on Thry all the time gets old," Xylo said, almost to himself rather than for Melt's edification. Everyone knew of Xylo's transporting deficiency, but no one was stupid enough to remind him of it.

"So . . . what is the official count?" Xylo asked.

Melt gathered himself and straightened up. "Forty-seven total."

"Three more since the last time?"

"Yes, sir."

"Who got them? Ranthis?"

"No, sir. Thansas."

"Thansas captured all three?"

"Yes, sir — single-handed."

"I assume Fingust has him after another?"

"Yes, sir."

"Good."

Xylo walked to the front of the Liqwall and looked at it,

smiling dryly. He put his finger into the clear, gooey substance. "Quite the creation," he whispered.

"Yes, sir."

"But only forty-seven — a little less than half our prey. Not very good for all these years, wouldn't you agree, Melt?"

"Yes, sir."

"And wouldn't you also agree that until we have the Book of Light, we cannot complete our conquest of the Brilliants?"

"I would agree, sir. However, even if and when we get the Book of Light, we still must face the Brilliants in their own territory, and getting in and then out is not going to be easy."

Xylo turned and stared at Melt, his eyes completely black as his thin eyebrows raised slowly. "It won't be easy, especially if we face the Colossals, but my plan will work."

"Sir?"

"What we need is a Musicular."

"But there hasn't been a Musicular for . . ." Melt started.

"I know, Melt. But one will emerge eventually."

"But isn't the Robe at the Lighthouse, sir?"

Xylo floated close to Melt. "Even if he is there, we shall defeat him."

"But, sir, you . . . "

Melt caught himself.

"Go ahead, Melt. You may speak freely."

"Sir, you've fought him only one time since I've served you, and he almost destroyed everything. He took so much."

"Indeed. But his weakness is his caring for the Brilliants. I will use that to bring him down," Xylo said, turning back to the Liqwall.

"Yes, sir," Melt said quietly.

There was a long pause before Melt spoke again.

"Sir, I've been meaning to ask about Mathias Braxton. Thansas has mentioned him many times. We could use his power, sir."

"Mathias Braxton? Yes, with the Gift of Manipulation. I remember the boy and his parents. The Brilliants have been wise to keep him hidden from us, no doubt in the Lighthouse. But it might be worthwhile to find out more about the boy and see if there's something we can use to draw him out. You are to talk with Fingust, and have him assign Water and Fury to find out as much as they can."

"What about Taker, sir?"

"No. He already has a job."

"But, sir . . ."

"No, Melt. Taker's powers are limited, and I would only send him if we knew where the boy was."

"As much as I loathed them, it was a great loss when Strength, Speed, and Imagination were defeated," Melt said angrily. "The problem is that those powers are irreplaceable until the Weavers repair the Vests and send them back down, and who knows when that will be."

"Why my brother actually showed himself is still a wonder to me." Xylo turned and breathed deeply, floating higher. "Never before has he come to the aid of a Brilliant directly like he did that day in the barn."

A knock came from behind them, and Xylo floated over to the door. He motioned with his finger, and the large, stone door slid open.

"Xylo, sir, we just discovered a new Brilliant," the young teenage boy said very quickly and nervously.

"What's the Gift?"

"The Gift of Speed, sir."

"Ah —" Xylo looked at Melt, smiling. "The Weavers are quicker than we give them credit for."

In a blast of black light, Xylo transported both Melt and the messenger boy to a small, circular room carved out of a cavern wall into which forty-inch computer screens were embedded.

At each of the ten windows, there was a Dark Vest watching intensely. The messenger boy motioned his leader over to a muscular girl who sat glued to one of the screens.

She sensed Xylo and stood up immediately. "Sir," she said, stepping aside.

Xylo looked into the window slowly.

"You're sure it's Speed?" he asked muscle girl while keeping his eyes on the screen.

"We've been monitoring him for some time, and I assure you it is Speed, sir."

Xylo stroked his cheek slowly. "We have a new Speed it seems. We need that power. Where does the boy live?"

"Washington state, sir."

Xylo looked surprised. "You're sure?"

"Yes, sir," said muscle girl in a monotone.

"Strange that so much is happening in Washington. Melt, I want you to send Kelvin and Sickle. Tell them to use Thry to get them there. I want that boy captured and brought here."

"As you wish, sir." Melt paused. "Do you wish to send Tidan, sir?"

"Tidan?" Xylo looked at Melt as though he had committed a most despicable act, even for him. "That fool couldn't help find water in a pool, let alone find this kid. I would've gotten rid of Tidan long ago had it not been for his power and protection."

"Yes, sir. Just a suggestion," Melt said quietly.

"And a bad suggestion at that."

THE ZOO

"Talk about the worst," George said, looking down at the map on the folded brochure. "How are we supposed to get this done in two hours? Look at all of these questions."

George brought the clipboard up with his other hand and stared at the stapled packet that was attached.

"Question one — identify and classify the first set of animals found in the petting zoo area. Question two — what habitat is most suitable for the snow leopard, and what does her diet consist of here at Point Defiance Zoo and Aquarium? Question three — what species . . ."

"Will you give it a rest," Juan said, putting his hand on George's clipboard and pushing it away. "At least Mr. Higgins let us choose partners and you weren't stuck with Paul."

George's eyes shot across the grass and landed on Paul Hertzinger. Just like George and Juan, Paul was a seventh grader now, although how he passed sixth grade George and Juan never knew. Up until last year, Paul had been the biggest, meanest bully in the entire sixth grade class, at least until George and Juan followed Samantha's plan and knocked some humility into him at a dance last fall. Ever since, he'd been somewhat better but was still loathed by most of the students.

"Where's . . ." George asked, looking around the crowded entrance lawn.

"I'm right here," Samantha replied, walking up behind him.

Samantha Banks was gorgeous. Last year she had been beautiful, but according to Juan and George's friends, this year she was gorgeous, which meant very little to George and Juan. They didn't look at Samantha that way, mostly because the three friends had grown up together and were more like sister and brothers.

Samantha's hair had grown longer and now the slightly curled mass hung down to her waist. During the past year, she hadn't grown taller like Juan and George had. Rather, her height remained the same, but her body had filled out, and there was little mistaking that she was quickly becoming a woman.

During this same period, Juan had grown nearly four inches and bested George by an inch, something he loved to remind his friend about. And while Juan was getting taller, he was also getting thinner. His waist size had decreased considerably, and he was now wearing extra large shirts to accommodate his long upper body.

George also had a long upper body and was still fighting the red blotches on his jawline. Unlike Juan's short black fuzz, George's sandy hair was long and pulled back in a ponytail, which still drove his mother crazy.

"Aren't you going to cut that?" she would constantly ask, accompanied with comments like, "Your hair could use a good trimming."

"Come on, let's go," Samantha said, walking along the four-foot-wide cement sidewalk that carved through the lush, green grass.

Juan and George followed, each equipped with a pencil, a clipboard, and a nine-page packet that had to be completed in the couple of hours they had to spend at the zoo. Point Defiance Zoo and Aquarium was one of two major zoos found in Washington state. Run by the city of Tacoma, the zoo was a mecca for kids and adults alike to get a chance to see animals of all sorts. It was the third week of September, the third week of classes at Eagle Crest Middle School, and it was Mr. Higgins who'd arranged for his science class to take a field trip to the zoo . . . the only class that George, Samantha, and Juan shared.

"I'm surprised you're not with Aerial," Samantha said as

she walked along the cement path toward the elephants.

"Shut up," George said from behind, trying to read the questions on the clipboard and walk at the same time.

"Well, only because you two were sitting on the bus and everything," Samantha said sarcastically.

"You're just jealous," George snapped.

Samantha stopped and wheeled around.

"Oh, man," Juan said, wearing a here-we-go-again look on his face.

"Jealous of what? Jealous because you have a girlfriend, and I don't have a boyfriend? Huh? I'll have you know that I could have a boyfriend . . . if my dad said I could go out," Samantha said, albeit progressively slower as she neared the end of her sentence.

"We're not going out! Everybody keeps saying that. We're just friends," George countered, pushing the paper down on the clipboard and staring at Samantha. "Just friends," he emphasized.

"It's not like you have to explain yourself or anything." Samantha waved her hand. "It's your business."

"Right. Can we move on then?" Juan attempted.

"Yes, please," George said longingly.

"George," called a sweet voice, "are you coming with us?"

It was Aerial Sampson, the blond-haired beauty, now in eighth grade. She was, coincidently, a teacher assistant for Mr. Higgins' first period class, which meant that she had to tag along with the seventh graders for the field trip.

George looked quickly at Juan, who gave him a no-big-deal shrug. George then looked at Samantha and received a you're-not-even-thinking-about-going look.

"Hmm . . . Aerial, I'm going to stay with Juan and Manthers. Sorry."

Aerial was standing with Sabrina Jersey and Nicole Jackson on the cement path below and when she heard his answer, did not look pleased. She glared at him and then bent close to whisper something to Sabrina and Nicole.

"You can go with her," Juan said supportively.

"I know. I don't want to."

"Liar," Samantha said, and then smiled. "I was just giving you a hard time. You can go with her if you want."

"Thanks, Manthers, but I really don't want to. She's been," George went into a whisper, "drivin' me nuts. She's calling me all the time, wanting me to go with her to the mall. I like to shop and stuff, but to just sit around in the mall all day — no thanks."

Juan began to laugh. "You're the man."

The two boys gave each other five.

"Girls," Juan continued sardonically and in a much higher octave. "Let's go to the mall and hang out. Give me a break."

"Why I spend my time with you two — I wish Kristina had this class," Samantha grunted.

"Oh, sorry," came George's flat, rather sarcastic response. "I'll bet Paul would love to have you work with him."

The boys exchanged another five.

"Funny," Samantha said, and turned around abruptly, continuing toward the elephants.

The zoo, for the most part, was outdoors, and the bright, cloudless September day made it enjoyable. Samantha, George, and Juan made their way to the gated elephant area where three large African elephants lumbered around a nature set, complete with a running brook and large pool in which the giant animals could bathe.

"Okay, okay," George said, flipping through his packet. "Elephants . . . I know I saw a page on elephants."

"Page seven, question three," Samantha said, her head buried in the packet as well.

"Oh!" Juan said, reading the question. "How are we supposed to know this? We're going to have to ask someone who works with the elephants this question."

"No, we're not," George said coolly.

Juan looked at George who nodded toward Samantha. Wrapped around her upper body was the brilliant white and gold color of her Vest — the Vest of Knowledge. It had been a year ago since the three had decided to explore Boulder Cave that late Sunday afternoon in September — a year ago since they discovered a Chest; an old, weather-beaten Chest in one of the large caverns within the grotto — a year since George opened it — a year since the white smoke filtered out of it and a blinding light shouted:

To you, the Gift of Flight.

To you, the Gift of Invisibility.

To you, the Gift of Knowledge.

It had been a year since their lives, their dreams, and their friendship were changed forever.

"What are you doing?" Juan hissed, looking around to make sure that no one would hear. "We agreed a long time ago that we wouldn't use our powers in school."

"I know," Samantha said, writing the answer down on the paper. "But I want to enjoy the zoo, not worry about all these questions. Besides, technically, I'm not in school."

This made sense to George because he was copying down what Samantha had written, and it didn't take long before Juan was doing the same.

"It's so awesome that you can just know stuff, like that," George said, snapping his fingers.

"Would you want to trade powers?" Samantha asked. "You know, if you could, would you trade? You could have Knowledge and I could have your Gift of Flight."

"Would you?" George retorted.

"I asked you first." Samantha smiled.

George thought about it a moment, biting his lower lip. "No, it's too cool to fly. You?"

"No."

"What about you, Juan?" George asked.

"I wouldn't trade mine for either of yours. Not now anyway. There was a time, though, when I was scrubbing toilets for Mr. Shields that I thought this was the worst Gift ever, not to mention the fact that Josh Zimmerman almost sat down on me in the toilet."

A woman approached them from behind, pushing a bald-headed boy, maybe six years old, in a wheelchair. Walking alongside him was a gray-haired woman that Samantha knew right away was the boy's grandmother.

The boy in the wheelchair, Jayden, (Samantha's Vest was telling her) was thin and very pale. His large blue eyes had purple rings around them as if he hadn't slept in a very long time. His mother and grandmother, although smiling, looked just as tired and run-down.

"The elephants, Mommy," the boy cried excitedly.

"That's right, the elephants," his mother said happily. "Excuse us. Could we maybe squeeze in between the three of you?"

"Yeah, no problem," Juan said as he and George moved out of the way so that the mother could push the boy to the fence, his grandmother at his side, holding his hand. Samantha stood frozen, her face contorted with a look of sadness and confusion.

"Hi," the boy said, looking up at her. "These are elephants."

Samantha nodded slowly, looking as though she was about to cry.

"I like elephants. My mom says that I can spend the day at the zoo, and afterward she's taking me to get some ice cream," the boy said innocently.

Samantha nodded again but said nothing. The lights of her Vest shot back and forth, but only Juan and George could see its brilliance.

"Samantha, we need to go to the next spot," Juan called nervously as he watched Samantha, who was still staring at the boy.

"I can't see them very good, Mommy. Please, Mommy. Can I stand up? I want to walk."

"No, no." His mother moved to the side of the wheelchair. "Oh, honey. No, I can't pick you up. Remember the surgery?"

The boy reached up to his grandmother.

"Grandma can't either, honey. You've got to stay in the chair."

"But, Mom," the boy coughed roughly. "Okay."

"Uh, Samantha — " George called.

This seemed to break Samantha out of the trance she was in because she finally backed away toward George and Juan.

"What are you doing? You were just —" but George stopped speaking when he saw the first tear fall. "What is it?"

"That boy has cancer, really bad. I don't think he has very long to live. And his mom and grandma love him so much. They wanted to do something for his birthday, so they brought him here to the zoo. He wants to see the animals, but he can't see them very well because he's in that chair. All he wants to do is see the animals."

Something inside George welled up like a great balloon and immediately a golden Vest of Light emerged over his blue, short-sleeve shirt.

"Now what are you doing?" Juan frowned.

"I'm going to help that boy see better," George said in a whisper, his eyes glistening with compassion.

And then, before Samantha and Juan could tell him differently, he soared into the air, twenty feet above them, and flew until he was hovering above the large elephants and facing the boy in the wheelchair.

It seemed like everything just stopped, as though time

didn't continue. Juan and Samantha were frozen, their mouths open in shock as George descended toward the young boy.

"Oh my," Jayden's mother gasped, pulling the wheelchair back.

"Don't be afraid," George said kindly. "I just want to help your son. He wants to see better, so I thought he'd like to take a ride around with me."

The boy's mother looked utterly flabbergasted. His grandmother looked as though she might faint, and there were a few kids doing double takes as they walked past and saw George hovering magically.

"Please —" George grew closer. "I won't hurt him."

George changed from an upright, vertical position, to his favorite, horizontal Superman position. He lay still, hovering directly in front of the young boy. Without a word and very quickly, Jayden raised himself up and crawled onto George's back, straddling him like a horse and burying his hands tightly in George's shirt.

"Jayden," his mother gasped in desperation.

"It's okay, Mommy. He's a good boy."

"Please," his mother said, her eyes brimming with tears.

George turned his head and looked at the boy out of the corner of his eye. "My name's George. Do you wanna see the zoo from higher up?"

"Okay," Jayden shouted, every tooth showing in his wide smile.

Slowly, ever so slowly, George Luisi ascended into the air and over the elephants so that he was only a few feet above them. Children and adults were beginning to crowd along the fence, their double takes now unbelievable stares — a teenage boy with a six-year-old on his back — flying.

George glided over to one of the elephants near the water and hovered. Jayden was laughing and pointing. A feeling of great joy was overtaking George, and he found himself smiling just as much as the boy suffering from cancer on his back.

The elephant nearest the water turned its head up to George and Jayden and let out a loud bellow, raising its trunk so that it touched George's stomach. George descended closer, and the elephant, as though it knew what George was hoping it would do, pushed the tip of its trunk against Jayden's chest. The boy laughed, rubbing the trunk as the elephant prodded his belly gently. Another one of the elephants nearest the water lumbered over into the large pool, dipped its trunk into it, and then spewed water into the air, soaking George and his young rider. Jayden held out his hands and caught the water as it came down like rain, laughing and shouting, "More, more." The elephant obliged. By the third dip and spew, the two boys were thoroughly drenched.

By now, a massive group of people had crowded along the fence, shouting, pointing, and enjoying the unbelievable spectacle. Some people were taking pictures, and kids everywhere were calling, "Over here, over here," as though George was a ride, and they were going to be next.

George floated higher, and as he did, all three of the elephants raised their trunks and let out a chorus of noise that George could've sworn sounded like good-bye. He made his way back to the boy's mother and grandmother, who stood, tears streaming down their faces, amidst looks of great delight.

"Mommy, did you see that?" Jayden shouted. "Did you see?"

"I saw it, honey," his mother whispered.

"Can I see the rest of the zoo with George — please, Mommy?"

Jayden's mother looked at George compassionately.

"It's okay. You can follow along as we go," George said reassuringly.

Jayden's mother nodded.

George turned his head and looked at Jayden. "What's next?

How about over there to the reindeer area?"

"Okay," Jayden said happily.

"Excuse me," a rough voice called out from the crowd as a red-haired woman, wearing a maroon Point Defiance Staff shirt pushed her way through the crowd. "You need to come down. This kind of behavior is not permitted in the . . ."

The woman couldn't finish as she watched George soar high above her. "No offense, but this boy's going to see the park with me today," George said with a certain power that neither Samantha nor Juan had ever heard before. He was definitive and strong, and there wasn't any way the zoo employee was going to interfere with Jayden's aerial tour.

"What's he doing?" Juan said, pointing as George flew his way over to the gated-off reindeer enclosure. "How is he going to explain this? He's flying!"

The crowd of people followed him, leaving Samantha and Juan alone. Samantha turned to Juan quickly. "Go invisible."

"Huh?"

"Go invisible," Samantha said forcefully.

"Why?"

"You never know, we might need you. Go — turn now. There's nobody looking."

In an instant, Juan was invisible.

"Let's follow the crowd, but from a distance," Samantha said to the air where she thought Juan was.

"Okay," came his reply.

The next half hour was incredible — incredible not only for Jayden, his mother and grandmother, but for George and everyone else who followed, gawking and pointing at the flying boy and his young friend. If that weren't enough, it seemed as though every animal in the zoo knew what George was trying to do and were somehow attempting to give Jayden's experience a personal touch. Like when the reindeer galloped around the pasture together in unison; or when the lazy snow leopard jumped out from behind the shade of a large boulder, climbed a dead, leafless tree in the center of its pasture, and held its paw for Jayden to shake, which the boy did without hesitation.

Then there were the water buffalo that snorted and frolicked around in their mud pool, the polar bears that actually waved at them as they passed overhead, and the sea otters who did fantastic water acrobatics — all of it to the delight of Jayden, George, and the crowd that followed their every move.

But it was when George soared over the dolphin pool that the scene became even more incredible. In a gigantic pool of seawater, some twenty feet below the flying boys, swam one dolphin and a beluga whale. As soon as George began to float over the center of the water, the dolphin began doing amazing tricks, exploding out of the water into twirls and flips. The whale joined in by torpedoing across the top of the water, back and forth, then diving down deep before coming to the top like a submarine surfacing, shooting a stream of water into the air and soaking the already drenched boys.

George had no idea it was Jayden's intention, but as Samantha looked on from a distance, she knew what was going through his mind. She whispered loud enough for Juan, who stood invisible next to her, to hear.

"He's going to jump in there with the dolphin."

She had barely finished the sentence when, to the gasps of the crowd, Jayden fell into the invitingly clear blue water. George couldn't believe it. What was the boy thinking? He saw Jayden's body plunge deep into the water and made a quick move to dive after him, but then stopped as the dolphin shot toward the boy and hoisted him on top of its back. When Jayden surfaced, he was clutching the top of the dolphin's fin tightly, riding it just as he had done with George . . . and loving every second. The crowd that had stood temporarily dumbfounded began to applaud, and Jayden began to laugh. Back and forth and around in circles the dolphin went, with the whale at its side, pushing through the water with ease.

George smiled and watched from his position as Jayden rode and rode, and the crowd cheered, and his mother and grandmother cried tears of happiness. This went on for a long time before the dolphin swam to the center of the pool, and Jayden looked above him, holding his hands up toward George, who descended and allowed Jayden to get back on.

Jayden was laughing, George was laughing — anyone who had been there that day would've laughed, too, because it was funny — it was special.

"Thanks so much," Jayden said gratefully as George flew back to the cement trail where the crowd of people, including Jayden's mother and grandmother, stood waiting.

George hovered close to the ground, and Jayden climbed off, greeted immediately by his mother's hug.

"Mom, that was so fun!"

His mom nodded, but said nothing as tears flowed. A dripping George stood up and faced the crowd. Kids of all ages, students from his own school — even adults — stared at him in awe. Jayden gave his mother a kiss and sat down in his wheelchair as his grandmother rubbed his wet head gently, murmuring, "Special boy . . . special boy."

"I don't know who you are or what power you have, but I do know," Jayden's mother said in a whisper, "that you have made this day a great day for my only son."

George was speechless as she took him in her arms and hugged him.

"Thank you, thank you. God has surely blessed you."

George pulled away and fought back the tears. Kids stepped forward from every direction begging him to take them on a ride. Three park employees in maroon shirts were pushing their way through the crowd, each with a very unhappy face and staring at George. People were crowding around so tightly that even Jayden and his mother couldn't get out. Despite numerous attempts, George could sense that the situation was quickly becoming chaotic.

The crowd pushed George back into the guardrail that lined the cement trail. He was about to go airborne when something very strange happened. The mass of people, except for Jayden, his mother, grandmother, and George, took one huge, collective leap ten feet backward as if they had been pushed by a giant hand. Then the group shifted again and parted down the middle, allowing Jayden and his family through easily. The people crowded together were shouting, unable to move.

"Mommy, turn around," Jayden said as his mother pushed him up the sidewalk.

She turned the wheelchair slowly until he was facing George.

"Thanks again, George. And I like your Vest . . . it's cool."

George's mouth fell open.

"Okay, Mom. We can go now."

Jayden's mom wheeled him around and up the cement trail until they turned the corner and disappeared. George began searching for Samantha and Juan when a bright flash of light exploded next to him. When the brilliant burst had dissipated, a teenage girl with golden blond hair that hung to the middle of her back in two large braids was standing beside him. Around her chest was a sparkling Vest of Light.

"Hi, George," she said kindly. "My name's Jazmin."

"Uh . . . hi."

"We need to fix a few things here," she said, reaching down into her jeans pocket and pulling out what looked like a golden golf ball pulsing with a bright white light.

George stared at the faces in the crowd who were now even louder than ever, all of them stuck as though they were nailed to the ground.

"What is that?" George asked, pointing to the golden orb.

"A Forgetter."

"A what?"

"A Forgetter," Jazmin said casually as if George should've known.

"What is it?"

"It's a ball that makes you forget. When I smash it to the ground, everyone who saw you fly today and the miraculous things that happened will forget," Jazmin said, bringing the ball to her lips and whispering something.

"You can't do that. Jayden and his mom . . ."

"Don't worry. They'll be able to remember, and so will you. I just don't need everyone else to remember." She reached into her other pocket and pulled out another ball, this one the same size as the Forgetter, only blue in color. "This is a Retriever — it works on small objects."

"Uh-huh," George uttered incoherently.

Jazmin laughed. "Let's do the Retriever first."

She brought the blue ball to her lips, whispered something again, and threw it to the cement. When it exploded, a whirlpool of blue light grew four feet tall and black objects came shooting from every direction into it. It took George a few seconds before he realized that the black objects were cameras. When the last one had been sucked into the whirlpool, it exploded into a great flash of blue. Jazmin then threw the golden ball down against the ground. White light shot out everywhere and was so intense, George had to shut his eyes.

"That should do it," Jazmin said with a smile.

The people who had been rooted in place now moved away from each other, muttering things, wondering what they were doing there in the first place. While everyone dispersed, Jazmin and George stood still until they were finally alone.

George's Vest had disappeared, but Jazmin's was still as bright as ever. Then George remembered about his two friends. "Samantha . . . . Juan . . . they were around here. They saw me fly, and you used that Forgetter."

"It's okay," said Jazmin calmly. "I transported them before I came to you. They remember everything. They're waiting for us, so shall we?" Jazmin gestured with her hands, opening her palms.

"Shall we what?" George said slowly.

"Transport."

"Transport?"

"Yes," said Jazmin. "Transport. On the count of three. One, two . . ."

"I don't think . . ."

". . . three."

In a blink, George was standing on a high plateau overlooking a large body of water. He turned, and standing only a few feet from him were Juan and Samantha. Next to them stood Jazmin, another girl whom George had never seen before, and a tall man he did not recognize, either.

"How'd it go?" the man asked, turning to Jazmin.

"Just fine, Lance. They worked."

"Good. That's a relief. Last time we tried to use a Forgetter, everyone ended up crawling on the ground like babbling babies."

"Told you they'd work," the girl named Evenina said, smiling at Lance.

"What's going on?" George asked, looking completely baffled. Samantha and Juan looked just as confused.

"You've got some questions, I'm sure," Jazmin said, brushing her long bangs away from her face. "So, why don't we sit down and see if we can answer some of them for you."

Jazmin pointed behind them where, arranged in a semicircle, were six white lawn chairs. She was the first to sit down, followed by Lance and Evenina. Samantha, Juan, and George joined them a bit reluctantly.

"First, where are we?" George asked.

"You're on a ridge overlooking the Pacific Ocean on the big

island of Hawaii. I figured you'd want a warm place to get dry, George," Jazmin answered.

"How did you get us here?" Samantha asked.

"Concentrate on your Vest," Evenina, the dark-haired, dark-skinned girl said.

Samantha donned her Vest and smiled. "You're Jazmin and you have the Vest of Transport, which gives you the ability to transport objects and people just about anywhere."

"Good job," Jazmin said with a nod. "What about the rest of us?"

Samantha turned to Evenina. "You're Evenina Farias. And you have the power of telekinesis."

"Tele — what?" asked a bewildered George.

"Telekinesis. She's able to move objects," replied Samantha.

"Good." Evenina smiled.

"That explains it." George clasped his hands together. "It was you that made the people back away from me, wasn't it? You were using your power to push them back?"

"Right."

"Cool power. And you made them part down the middle so that Jayden could get by?"

"Right."

"Where were you?" George wondered.

"Behind the crowd of people," Evenina answered quietly.

"Didn't even see you."

Samantha continued her analysis as she stared at Lance. He was fair-skinned with a head of thick, light brown hair neatly combed and parted. His green eyes were deeply set, and when he smiled, a dime-sized dimple formed on each cheek.

"You're Lance Christopher. You have the Gift of Communication. You can speak to and understand animals."

"What?" Juan looked very intrigued. "You can talk to animals?"

"Yes. Why do you think the animals were acting like that in the zoo? I was asking them to make it special for that little boy, and they obliged, quite willingly."

"So that was it —" George sighed. "The dolphin . . . that was awesome."

"Yeah, that dolphin is awesome, even though she hates being cooped up in that pool. She does like the company of the beluga, though."

"That's amazing. You can communicate with any animal?" Juan marveled.

"Right. Just about any of them. There are a few that don't respond sometimes, but for the most part they all do," answered Lance.

"All of you are Brilliants," Samantha said, her Vest still glowing brightly.

"Just like you." Jazmin pointed to her. "We're Envoys sent to take you to the Lighthouse to start your training."

"Training?" George blurted.

"The Maker feels it's time for you to begin learning more about your Gifts and how your powers work."

"Wait, wait. What about Mr. Higgins? He's going to freak," George said, now looking panicked.

"Don't worry. Tristen will take care of that for you. You won't be going to school for a while now. At least not the kind of school you're used to," Evenina said.

"Who's Tristen?" asked George.

"He takes care of things like this for us. He's been doing it for years. Trust us. He'll get everything in order for you at school."

"Before we take you to the Lighthouse," Jazmin said, "do you have any other questions?"

"I have one," Juan said. "There are more Vests, right?"

"Yes," Jazmin answered.

"And they have different powers?"

"Yes. Some powers are similar to others, but they are all different."

"Have you ever faced any of the Dark Vests?" George jumped in.

"Yes," Jazmin, Evenina, and Lance answered in unison.

"Are there a lot of them?"

"Unfortunately . . . yes," Lance answered slowly.

"We fought them, too, last year in a barn . . ." Juan started.

"We know all about that. It's legend how you fought and how the Robe came to help you." Lance smiled gently. "None of the Brilliants except for the Maker and Defense have ever seen the Robe, so you three are famous, not to mention special."

"Special?" Samantha raised her eyebrows.

"The Robe has never helped any of the Brilliants, except for maybe the Maker at the beginning. So the fact that he saved you, makes you all unique."

"Who is the Maker?" asked George.

"The leader of the Brilliants."

"What's his power?"

Jazmin let out a long sigh before answering. "He's able to make just about anything."

"What? Anything?" George couldn't believe it.

"Right. He's the oldest of all the Brilliants, besides the Robe, and he's one of the most powerful," Evenina said seriously.

"This is incredible," cried Juan.

"Oh, it gets better," Jazmin added. "I think we're ready for the Lighthouse, don't you?"

Lance and Evenina nodded.

"Get ready . . . here we go."

"Fingust," Melt said, louder this time as he stared at the enormous stone door.

He waited.

"Fingust, open the door."

There was no response. He'd been standing in front of this door for almost five minutes.

"I'm going to count to five, you old man, and if I get to five and this door isn't open, I'll melt it to nothing."

Silence.

"One." Melt paused. Maybe the old man's dead, he thought. No, impossible. Fingust was too old to die. He just liked being belligerent.

"Two."

Pause.

"Three."

No response.

"Four."

He waited. Again, no response.

"Five."

Nothing.

"Fine." Melt raised his hands, while the sparkles of black danced around his Vest. In just a few seconds, the stone door had been completely liquefied. Melt walked into the room, being careful not to step in the hot, gooey material that had, a few moments before, been the door. Fingust was sitting in a chair, staring down at a computer screen that was embedded into the stone desk. The old man didn't bother to look up.

"Fingust, what do you think you're doing?" Melt shouted in reference to the locked door. "I know you heard me, you dinosaur."

Fingust didn't acknowledge him.

"I'm talking to you!"

"Yes, so you are," the old man spoke in his strange, gargled voice, finally looking up at the furious Melt.

Fingust was ancient. No one actually knew his exact age except Xylo. Many of the Dark Vests speculated that he was well over a hundred and attributed his long life to the fact that his Gift, the power he had received from a Chest of Light, was the power to heal.

"Why do you insist upon not answering me?" Melt asked, disgusted.

Fingust curled his upper lip, as he did anytime he was agitated. His thin-lipped face was decorated with wrinkles and extra chins, along with a completely bald head. His eyes were set far back in his skull, and his nose looked off-center, as though someone had twisted it to the far left of his face. When he spoke, he took strange, intermittent breaths and sounded as though he was gargling a build up of saliva.

"I don't answer you, Melt, because I don't like you," Fingust slurred.

"I don't care if you like me or not! I have orders from Xylo. You are to find the following Vests: Kelvin . . . "

Fingust stood up suddenly. "Get out."

"What?"

"I only take orders directly from Xylo, not from psychos like you."

Melt laughed. "It was Xylo who instructed me to tell you that we need to get in contact with some of the Vests."

"I've never taken orders from you," the old man spat.

"Things change, Fingust. Now, you need to . . ."

"I don't see why I have to listen to you . . ."

Melt's patience was gone. He raised his right hand as sparkles of black appeared around his fingertips. Fingust suddenly let out a frightful, ear-splitting scream and watched as his left arm began to dissolve into liquid bone and flesh. The pain nearly caused him to pass out, but not before he donned his Vest and concentrated. Nearly as fast as his arm had melted, Fingust restored it back to normal.

"All right. All right," he cried, rubbing his newly formed bicep with his other hand.

"Don't ever forget who you're dealing with, Fingust," Melt said, lowering his arm and staring at the old man with pure hatred.

From behind Melt, a bald, brown-skinned man entered. He had a massive chest and arms the size of most people's legs. His lips were squeezed together, and he looked very serious. He spoke with a deep, resonating voice.

"What's going on?"

Melt didn't bother to turn around. He knew who it was. "This isn't your concern, Raxban."

"What was all that screaming?" Raxban stood next to Melt, examining Fingust carefully.

"He melted my arm!" the old man snarled.

"Deserved it, you senile old fool," Melt shot back.

"Deserved it?"

"Shut up, Fingust. You probably did deserve it, you freakin' fossil. He should've melted more than just your arm."

Melt smiled wickedly. Raxban turned and grinned as well before leaving the room.

"What do you need?" Fingust stammered, trying to sound suddenly cheerful as he sat back down in the wooden chair behind his desk.

"I need you to get Kelvin, Sickle, Water, and Fury, as well as Thry."

"That might take a few minutes. Kelvin is in Japan. I haven't heard from him in a month."

"He's still looking there? He'll never find it — should've put

Malavax on it. No matter now. We need him back."

"That might take some time."

"Hurry it up. Xylo wants him back as soon as possible."

"What's all this for?" the old man said, turning his attention back to the computer screen. Melt didn't answer.

Fingust pressed the screen buttons and watched intently. "Kelvin isn't responding — typical of him, really. He hardly ever answers."

Fingust looked up and cracked a smile.

Melt was expressionless.

"Continuing on. . . ." Fingust moved his eyes back to the screen. The next few minutes were silent — something that Fingust was beginning to dislike more and more. Small beads of sweat formed in the thick wrinkles of his forehead. Finally appearing on the screen was the face he was seeking.

"Water."

"Fingust? What is it? I'm busy," came a low voice.

"Melt is here and informs me you need to get here as soon as possible. Xylo has a new job for you."

Water's real name was Dale DeMarco. He was sixteen, although his dark skin and hefty build caused people to mistake him for a twenty-five year old. He had short, spiked hair. He looked dismayed when Fingust told him he was to return.

"Fine. How am I going to get back?" he asked, setting something down that he'd been carrying. Fingust tried to see what it was, but it was out of view. Fingust looked up to Melt.

"Thry will pick him up," Melt responded.

"Thry will pick you up," Fingust echoed into the screen.

"When?"

Fingust looked up again.

"When she finds you. Just be ready," Melt shouted so that Water could easily hear.

"Is that you, Melt?"

"Yes, you idiot. Xylo needs you back here, so be ready. Thry will pick you up within the next couple of days."

"Yes, fine," Water said, subdued.

"Move on," Melt commanded.

The old man touched the screen and Water disappeared. It would take a few more minutes before another man appeared. It was Fury, whose real name was Frank Vaughn.

"What is it?" Fury asked, perturbed. He looked like he had just gotten up. His brown hair was a thick, tangled mop and the imprint of his watch was embedded in his cheek.

"Melt has new orders for you."

"What?"

"Melt . . . he has new orders for you," Fingust repeated.

"Yeah, okay. What are they?" Fury said, brushing his hand across his face.

"Don't worry about the details, Fury. Just have your stuff ready because I'm sending Thry to get you."

"Okay," Fury said, shutting his eyes as if trying to get a last minute wink of sleep.

"Lazy," Melt said in an annoyed voice. "Move on, Fingust."

The very old man pressed a button on the screen and Fury disappeared. While Fingust continued touching the various buttons on the screen, Melt vented. "Bunch of fools. Why Xylo continues to keep some of these people is beyond me. We should melt the lazy and incompetent ones first."

Fingust looked over his shoulder, and couldn't help but think that he would be on the top of Melt's list. "I have Sickle," he said quietly.

Melt stared at the screen. In it was a striking, twenty-five-year old woman. Her dirty blond hair hung down over her shoulders in wavy curls. Her dark brown eyes and even darker skin were stunning.

"Melt?" she said, brushing the bangs out of her eyes. "What are you doing on the view screen?"

"Sickle — you're looking . . ."

"Gorgeous," she finished his sentence arrogantly. "You don't need to tell a goddess that she's gorgeous. She already knows."

Melt laughed heartily. Fingust rolled his eyes.

"You need to return to the Triangle. Xylo has another job for you."

"But I haven't completed the job here. I still have another week left."

"Don't care. Get back here. Conceal what you can. You can finish the job after you take care of what Xylo wants."

"And what does he want?"

"You'll get briefed when you get back. Thry will pick you up. Be ready. Keep going, Fingust."

"I'll see you soon, Melt," the woman said, pushing her lips together as though she was giving him a kiss.

The screen once again went dark as Fingust went to work, trying to locate Thry. Thry's real name was Vanessa Sarrels, an old, decrepit-looking woman, but who possessed one of the most important powers for the Dark Vests. Of them all, she alone possessed the power to translocate herself and others by using a porthole.

"Here she is." Fingust gestured to the screen.

"Thry, good to see you again."

"Hello, Melt. What do you need?" the old woman spoke slowly, her voice cracking.

"I need you to translocate Water, Fury, Sickle, and Kelvin."

"Soon?"

"Right away."

"Does Fingust have their coordinates?"

Fingust moved his head forward. "Yes, all except for Kelvin. I'll send them to you."

"Fine. Any particular order, Melt?"

"No."

Thry nodded. "I'll wait for their coordinates."

"I'm sending them to you now," Fingust said, punching

various keys. "When I eventually locate Kelvin, I'll send you his coordinates, too."

Melt walked out from behind Fingust and toward the melted entryway. He was almost out of the room when he turned and glared at the century-old man. "And the next time I knock, Fingust . . ."

"I'll answer promptly," Fingust gargled in a whisper.

"Very good."

Melt left the room and heard Fingust swear loudly. He had an inkling to go back in and threaten the old man, but he didn't have time. He had other business to take care of and decided he would let it slide this time.

Nearly everything in the Dark Triangle was lit by Eternal Flames — everlasting flames of various light that never needed attention. Melt turned left at a small junction and walked along the narrow passageway that led to a large, arched entrance. He entered and saw Ivory standing in front of a view screen embedded in the wall about six feet off the ground. She heard his footsteps but didn't turn around.

Melt made his way to the round, wooden table, and poured a glass of thick, greenish liquid from a pitcher into a large mug before sitting down on a wonderfully crafted, wooden rocking chair. He brought the cup to his lips, paused as he let the fragrance wander into his nostrils, and then gulped it down in two swallows.

"Ah," he said, wiping his mouth with the back of his hand. "That's good."

"Of course, Melt. You don't think I'm capable of making something poor, do you?"

The woman turned and winked at him. She was thirty years old, but looked much older. Her face was scarred and over her left eye was a patch — damage from a losing battle with a Laxintoth two years ago. She had her hair pulled back and concealed by the hood of her long robe. Her black skin glistened with the glow of the red Eternal Flames illuminating the room.

She walked toward him, her robe dragging along the rocky floor. "So, why the visit?"

"Xylo."

"What is it now?" she asked indignantly, her one brown eye squinting.

"There's a new Vest that we've been tracking."

"Really?" Ivory was interested. "Which one?"

"Speed."

"Speed?" She suddenly lost interest. "Impossible," she added, waving her hand nonchalantly.

"No, it's very possible. I've seen it. A boy."

"And you're sure it's Speed?"

"Positive," Melt said, getting up from the chair and pouring another glass of green syrup.

"The Weavers are working faster than usual. Argus hasn't been gone but a year. Usually it takes more time for the Weavers to make repairs."

"Yes, well," Melt took another gulp and sat down again, "I'm telling you, the Gift of Speed has returned."

Ivory was pacing now. "Just one power from the Chest?"

"Looks like it."

"Was there anything in the Chest?"

"I don't think so," Melt said calmly, sipping some more green.

"Are you sure?"

"Fairly sure."

The woman took a deep breath. "We need that boy. Speed was one of our greatest Gifts."

"Xylo has ordered his capture. It will only be a matter of time before we have him."

"Yes, but the problem is, can he be converted."

"He can, Ivory."

"You never know," she said, warningly. "I can tell you one

that cannot be converted."

She rubbed her hands together as if she was trying to make fire.

"Who?"

"Samantha."

"The girl with the Gift of Knowledge?"

"Yes."

"Why do you say that?" Melt got up for yet another refill.

"I've seen it," she whispered.

Ivory stood still and ran her eye back and forth across the room.

"Seen what?" Melt grunted.

"It is Samantha Banks who will emerge the leader of the Brilliants if we do not try and stop her now while she is still young."

"Relax. She's just a kid."

"NO!" Ivory shouted, pointing a finger at Melt. "Don't think that just because she's a kid, she's harmless. The Robe visited her and the other two for a very specific reason. He would not have done that if there wasn't something extremely important about her."

"I don't think we have to worry. Xylo is aware," Melt said casually.

Ivory resumed her brisk pace, walking in tight circles. "Samantha . . . Samantha Banks. Parents are Heidi and Michael. Her mother is a dental hygienist and her father is a teacher at a technical trade school."

"And this is important, why?" Melt was obviously not following.

Ivory ignored his question and continued. "The only daughter — has three older brothers. She grows stronger with her power and . . . and . . ."

"And what?"

"And they have found her."

Melt lowered the glass mug from his lips, waiting to take the last drink. "Who found her?"

"The Envoys," Ivory whispered. "She's going to learn about their world, and that makes her even more dangerous. It's her that Xylo should be going after first and foremost."

Ivory faced Melt nervously. "If Xylo neglects the fact that she is going to become more powerful, she will destroy us. She is the one that will succeed the Maker. She is the one I've seen who will unite the Brilliants against us."

Melt had forgotten about his mug of green. He was looking serious, just as serious as the woman in the room with him. He looked down at the floor and stared at his shiny, black boots and the strange shadows cast on them by the flickering of the Eternal Flames.

"I will tell Xylo," Melt finally said, breaking the brief silence. "How come you didn't tell me this earlier?"

"It wasn't becoming clear until now ——" she patted her chest where a Vest of Dark Light wrapped around her. "We need to stop her. Failure to get Samantha Banks will be catastrophic. She must be destroyed."

THE LIGHTHOUSE

The last thing George, Juan, and Samantha remembered seeing, at least seeing clearly, was light coming from Jazmin's hands. The next moment the three of them were surrounded by twirling blurs of yellow and gold. When everything finally stopped spinning, the first thing they noticed blaring off to the left was . . . earth.

Samantha opened her mouth to say something, but words escaped her. She had seen pictures in books and in movies of what earth looked like, but it was so different actually viewing it live from space. This immediately brought the realization: If I'm in space, I should be dead. There's no oxygen. How am I still alive?

"Pretty incredible, huh?" Jazmin pointed to the earth. "And the moon's just right there. Welcome to the home of the Brilliants. Welcome to the Lighthouse."

"Wait a second . . . wait a second. This, this . . ." George was pointing at the Lighthouse in the distance. "I had a dream about this place. Remember, you guys? I've seen this place before."

Juan was speechless. He, like Samantha, was awestruck. They were standing on a floor of light that shimmered and glistened with gold sparks everywhere. The luminescent carpet was enormous and seemed to go on forever. To the left, to the right — it was an endless sea of yellow and gold, and looming in the distance was a gigantic lighthouse.

Round and circular, the structure was made from light. Juan traced the front of it with his eyes and cranked his neck all the way back, but still couldn't see the top as it rose high into space. He tried to say something like "incredible" but just mumbled a few incoherent words.

"C'mon." Jazmin gestured them forward. "Let's go in."

Jazmin, Evenina, and Lance led the way while Samantha, George, and Juan took their time, staring in every direction, captivated that they were actually in space, hovering in between the earth and the moon. They approached the spectacular Lighthouse doors, forty feet tall and twenty feet wide. Standing at each side of the doors were, in Samantha's opinion, giants — half the height of the door, dressed in deep-blue armor. Even their eyes, which could barely be seen through their elaborate masks, were the same color.

Their suits of armor were all one piece, as if they had been tailor-made to fit their bodies. The mask was part of a tall helmet, at the end of which was a fluffy feather of the same color. The armor covered every part of their bodies, down to the gloves over their hands and the boots over their feet. Attached at the left shoulder was a glowing shield that emanated with the same intensity and color as a Vest of Light. Around their waist was a golden belt and attached to it was the longest sword any of the new Brilliants had ever seen. George, even with his wild imagination, couldn't have dreamed up swords like these, which glowed with an intense golden color, like that of the shoulder shield.

They all stood and watched as the giant on the right side pushed one of the massive doors open with a gentle touch of his finger. The ground shook violently for a few seconds as the door finally swung open all the way.

"Welcome," Jazmin said, stepping forward.

"What are they?" Samantha asked in wonder.

Jazmin turned. "They're Colossals."

"Colossals?"

"Protectors of the Lighthouse. They always guard the entrance — been here ever since the Maker built it."

"They've never left their post?"

"Not once. Maybe if you just use your Vest, it would tell you something about all of this."

Samantha looked down at her plain shirt. She had completely forgotten about her Gift of Knowledge, which was understandable considering everything that was happening. But this was nothing compared to what she, Juan, and George saw once they entered the Lighthouse with their Envoys.

In the center was a Fountain of light, and just like water, the light splashed and danced in the air before settling back down into a pool of liquid luminescence. About twenty feet above them, a boy, maybe eight or nine years old, floated over the fountain and smiled, before ascending up the open center that seemed to go on forever.

"Who was that?" George asked.

"I think it was Michael, wasn't it?" Lance asked Jazmin.

"I think so. He has the power to control wind. Young kid."

Samantha stood next to the Fountain and looked above her. She only had to wait a few seconds before another Brilliant floated across the center, high above her, and disappeared.

"This is a low gravity environment. Watch," Lance said, jumping in the air and floating above the Fountain. "The Lighthouse has seven levels, although you're only allowed to visit level one through six. The seventh is off-limits to most Brilliants."

"Why?" Juan mumbled, transfixed.

"That's always been the rule," Lance answered, setting back down on the lighted floor.

"Who's the Maker?"

Jazmin raised her arms. "The man that made this."

"He built it himself? He must be like those giants we saw outside the doors," George said.

"He's no giant, and he did make everything you see here. That's his power. He can make things, just like that." Jazmin snapped her fingers quickly.

"He can just . . . make things?" Juan said, almost whispering.

"Big and complex things take more time, but yeah, he makes things," Jazmin answered.

Juan shook his head.

"Why don't I take Juan and George to their rooms?" Lance suggested.

"Yeah, that sounds good. I'll take Samantha to her room and meet up with you later."

George and Juan followed Lance down a long corridor as Jazmin and Evenina guided Samantha in the opposite direction.

"The boys' quarters are down the other corridor and the girls' are down this one," Jazmin said casually.

"We have so much to teach you," Evenina added excitedly. "One of the first things is language. Believe it or not, you know every language in the world. One of the inherent gifts of all the Brilliants when they first receive their Vest is the ability to communicate with anyone whether we have our Vests on or not. It becomes a part of us. You know every language in the world, right now, right here, and you have since the day you got your Vest in Boulder Cave.

"Remember that not all the Brilliants come from English-speaking countries. There are Brilliants from all over the world, and we can all communicate with them. When they talk to you, you hear them speaking whatever your native tongue is. For you and me, that's English, but for someone whose native tongue is French, that's what they hear."

"Really?" Samantha said in awe.

"You'll see how it works as time goes on. And remember, you don't need your Vest to understand. The other great thing is that when you answer back, it seems like you're answering in your normal language, but to others who hear you speak, you're speaking in their native language."

"Whoa. So if I'm in like . . . Spain and I just see someone on the street and I ask them where the nearest store is, I'll actually be speaking Spanish, even though I hear English come out of my mouth?"

"Right, if Spanish is that person's primary lan-guage."

"But how will I know what their primary language is?"

"Won't matter. The power you have inside you will figure it out without you even thinking about it. It's one thing you actually don't have to concentrate on, which is nice since concentrating on your Vest all the time makes you tired, as I'm sure you've experienced," Evenina said.

"Oh yeah." Samantha nodded, admiring the balls of glowing light floating from the ceiling.

"That's the other thing that's really nice. Here in the Lighthouse, you'll never get fatigued, so you can keep your Vest on as much as you want," Jazmin added. "Test your Vest. What do you know about the Lighthouse that we haven't already told you?"

Samantha kept her eyes closed while Jazmin and Evenina watched intently. A few minutes passed in silence until Samantha's lips curled into a smile.

"Incredible," she whispered.

"Well?"

"The Lighthouse was built by the Maker because the Robe told him the Brilliants needed a meeting place — a headquarters. The Robe and the Maker are very close friends, like brothers."

"Good. Go on," Evenina said excitedly.

"We are on the first floor, which houses all the sleeping quarters and rooms where we stay."

"Excellent."

Samantha kept her eyes closed. "The second floor is the Banquet Hall, where we eat. The third floor is the briefing center, where we gather for important meetings. The fourth floor is the physical and mental training rooms. The fifth — the Music Room — and the Library is the sixth floor."

"And the seventh?" Evenina asked with a smile.

Samantha shook her head. "I don't know. I'm not getting anything."

"Hmm, interesting."

Jazmin and Evenina continued leading Samantha down the corridor. To her left and right were doors with no names and only a number on the front. Everything from the walls to the doors glistened with soft, white light.

Around a corner and into another hallway, the three walked until finally coming to the third door on the left, Room Thirteen. Jazmin stood in front of it for a moment and then moved away, gesturing for Samantha to stand where she had.

"There's no knob —" Samantha quickly observed.

"What does your Vest tell you to do?"

Samantha closed her eyes and almost immediately opened them again. Then she stepped through the door as though she were a ghost, passing completely through it and staring at a large open room, which reminded her of a luxurious hotel suite. To her immediate right was a spacious bathroom. In the center was a hot-tub-like bathtub. The entire tub as well as the faucets looked and sparkled like they were made of gold. Two long bath towels hung on one of the racks, while the wash cloths and hand towels were neatly stacked on a golden shelf adjacent to them. Samantha stepped forward to get a glimpse of the mirror that glowed with a brilliant white light and the sparkling faucets below.

She turned her attention to the rest of her quarters. Nestled against one of the walls was a sparking double bed — even the sheets glowed softly with light. Everywhere she looked objects were glowing. The round table and two chairs in the corner of the room — the eight-drawer dresser and mirror above it — even the closet doors in the other corner glowed softly. And just to her left, embedded in the wall, was a twenty-five-inch screen, very similar to a television screen. Samantha stepped closer and read the message in bold black letters on an all-yellow background:

Welcome to the Lighthouse, Samantha.

There was a knock, and Samantha remembered Jazmin and Evenina were still standing in the hallway. She turned and examined the door. Although there wasn't a handle, there was a small golden button in the center of it. She hesitated a moment and then pushed it. The door split in two, one end jetting off to the left and the other to the right.

Jazmin and Evenina stepped in quickly. "Forget about us?"

"I figured you could walk through the door, too."

"No. Only the owner of the room has that ability," Evenina stated matter-of-factly.

The doors closed behind them as Samantha turned her attention to the large glass window that overlooked the earth.

"How can this be? This huge Lighthouse orbiting the earth like it is?"

"Don't ask me. Ask your Vest."

Samantha thought for a moment. "All I get is the Maker."

"Exactly," Jazmin said. "He made it. How he did, however, is way beyond me."

"But hasn't it been detected by the space shuttle or something? It's not like you could hide this place."

Jazmin and Evenina laughed.

"Well?" Samantha turned, looking at Jazmin.

"You keep asking the wrong person, Samantha."

Samantha grinned and fell silent again. "All of this is invisible to anyone who doesn't have a Vest," she said slowly.

"Right."

"Clever. This Maker guy must have some imag-ination."

"Oh, wait until you meet him," said Evenina eagerly. "I've got to get to my room and change. I've been in these same clothes for two days."

"Yeah, you do. You were beginning to really stink," Jazmin

said sarcastically.

"Like you smell any better," Evenina joked.

"Where are your rooms?" wondered Samantha.

"Three doors down to the right. We share a room. Room Sixteen."

"You know, I don't have any of my clothes and things from my house —"

"Yes, you do," Jazmin said, as she made her way toward the door. Evenina followed as Jazmin pushed the golden button and the door split open again.

"No, I don't — really. All of it is at my house."

"No, it's not. We'll be back in a few minutes, and then we'll head up to the Banquet Hall to eat."

"But I need my things," Samantha said urgently, following Evenina and Jazmin to the door.

"They're already put away in the closet and the dresser. We'll see you in a few minutes," Jazmin said, walking away as the door shut behind her and Evenina.

Samantha turned and stared at the dresser. How could her clothes be here? She walked to the dresser and pulled open the first drawer. Underwear — hers. She looked around the room, feeling a bit embarrassed. She opened the second drawer — shirts — all neatly folded in small piles. Next drawer were pants. The entire dresser was full of her clothing from her bedroom at home. But how was that possible?

She moved to the closet and opened it up. Sure enough, hanging on golden hangers were a few of her dresses, along with a couple of jackets. She shook her head in disbelief.

"Amazing," she whispered to herself. "And what's this screen in the wall for?"

Immediately, her Vest gave her the answer. The screen was how everyone in the Lighthouse communicated. It acted like a videophone. To activate it, all she would have to do is say the name of the person she wanted to talk to, and that person would appear in the screen.

Samantha turned to the window that looked out into space. Outer space was something she figured she would never see up close. When she dreamed about what she wanted to be when she got older, an astronaut wasn't high on her priority list. But looking out her window and seeing earth, the moon, and the stars was breathtaking. She had never imagined it could be this spectacular.

For the next few minutes, Samantha simply stared, taking it all in. She wondered how Juan and George were doing, and if their rooms had a view like hers. Then came a knock on the door. She went to it, pushed the golden button, and the door opened. Evenina and Jazmin stood together dressed in fresh clothes.

"Let's get something to eat," Jazmin offered.

Samantha followed her to the Fountain while Evenina trailed behind. As they approached the splashing light, Jazmin jumped into the air and ascended into the open middle. Pushing off the ground, Samantha did the same.

The weightless feeling was exhilarating. She floated high above the Fountain and approached the second tier. Jazmin had already landed and watched as Samantha followed, trailed closely by Evenina. As Evenina touched down, a large, round-faced boy in a black wheelchair floated down from above and landed a few feet away.

"Jaz . . . Evenina," he said. "Who's the newbie?"

"Samantha Banks," Jazmin said.

"Hey, Samantha Banks — power of knowledge, chick?" The boy snapped his fingers.

"Right," Samantha said.

"The name's Fox, Fox Allen Thomas. I'm fat," he laughed at himself, putting his hands to his belly before extending his right hand to Samantha. Samantha's hand looked like an infant's compared to his as they shook. "Get it, F-A-T? My initials."

"Fox is really your name?" asked Samantha.

"Yep. Fox. The Fox. The Foxmeister. The Foxy . . . "

"Okay, we get the point, Fox," said Jazmin, slightly irritated.

"Right. Well, time for chow. I'll lead the way. If it's one thing I know, it's food."

The girls followed him down the corridor, which was lit with the same type of glowing balls as the first level. "This your first time?"

"First time?" Samantha wasn't sure what Fox meant.

"First time eating here?"

"Oh, yes."

"You're in for a treat. You've never had food like this before. Imagine your favorite things to eat. Are you doing that, 'cause it's rather important?"

Samantha glanced at Evenina and Jazmin as they walked. This Fox kid spoke so quickly, Samantha was sure his jaw was going to dislocate at any second.

"Are you imagining?"

"Yes, okay."

"Good, 'cause that's the key. It's not like we're gonna go and sit down and be served like in some restaurant. Can you image that? Heck no. This is the way we were meant to eat, don't you think?" Fox asked enthusiastically.

Samantha finally heard the boy take a long, deep breath. She figured she had about a second before he started again. "I really don't know."

The boy stopped and his wheelchair whipped around quickly. He was now looking very serious. "You haven't told her about eating?" he asked, looking at Jazmin unbelievably.

"Uh, no. Hadn't gotten there yet, Fox," answered Jazmin.

"Hadn't gotten to eating? Are you crazy? Look," he spoke, inspired, "this is the best, just the best. We're going to enter this huge hall and sit down. You're going to see a plate, a bowl, a big old glass, and utensils. There'll also be a thick glowing Belt. You put that Belt on before sitting down and then . . ." the boy could barely contain himself, ". . it begins. You *imagine* your food."

Samantha concentrated on her Vest quickly and tried to figure out exactly what imagining your food was, but nothing came to mind, so she reluctantly asked him, "What do you mean, you imagine your food?"

"Just like I said." Fox turned around and continued leading them down the corridor again. "You just imagine what you want to eat and boom! It appears on your plate or in your bowl. And it's real food. Real food! I think about pizza and BAM — it's there. You want spaghetti and meatballs, too? BAM —Salad? BAM! Mountain Dew to chase it down with — oh yeah, baby — BAM!" He clapped his hands together loudly. "And then dessert — think you want a piece of cake loaded with chocolate frosting — BAM! Whatever your little brain can actually think up, BA . . ."

"BAM!" Samantha finished, just as loud and obnoxious as he had been. This seemed to quiet him a bit.

"Right. You see, you're getting the hang of it. Here we are."

The view from the room that they entered was beautiful. Everywhere Samantha looked was an enormous window overlooking the celestial landscape. Aside from all of that, the room itself was quite simple. What looked like round, glass tables were scattered throughout the room. There must've been a hundred or so, and they, like everything else, glowed softly white. Even the chairs shimmered. Attached to each chair, like they were somehow magnetic, were the Belts Fox had mentioned.

Round balls of light hung about six feet over every table, illuminating the already bright room even more. The interesting thing about the balls, at least in Samantha's opinion, was that they seemed to be suspended over the tables without anything holding them up. There weren't any wires or strings. The balls of light simply floated.

"Hey, Fox," a boy said, brushing past them. He was tall and stocky with dark hair.

"Pete," Fox said, "where you sitting?"

Pete pointed to one of the tables next to one of the nearby windows. Three other boys were seated at the table, all of them with glowing Vests. Pete paused and looked at Samantha.

Samantha felt herself go red. Pete was quite handsome.

"You Samantha?"

"Yes," she managed to say weakly.

"Gift of Knowledge, right?"

"Yes."

"Someone told me you were coming. First day at the Lighthouse?"

"Yes."

Samantha was beginning to think she sounded like a skipping CD.

"Nice to meet you." Pete stuck out his hand and she shook it.

"You too," she said stiffly.

"You coming, Fox?" Pete asked, letting go of Samantha's hand and heading over to the table with the three boys.

"Yeah," Fox replied. "I'll talk to you later," he said, speaking to Jazmin, Evenina, and Samantha before wheeling off after Pete.

"Let's take the table over there by the far window," Jazmin said, leading Samantha and Evenina toward it.

They walked by three girls at one of the tables. Their plates were full of food. One girl had mashed potatoes and steaming gravy. Another had a large Belgium waffle smothered in strawberries and whipped cream. The third girl had a plate full of what looked like chicken and rice covered in a white cream sauce. All of it looked delicious.

At the table were plates stacked together, large mugs, and

an assortment of utensils, all of which glowed softly. Jazmin and Evenina each took a Belt from a chair and clasped them around their waists.

"Go on." Jazmin smiled. "Fox was right. Just put the Belt on and imagine what you want to eat — kinda like Peter Pan."

Samantha reached out and grabbed a Belt, pulling it away from the chair. It was lighter than it looked. She brought it around her waist, and it seemed to clasp together by itself, pulling snug without any effort on her part. She didn't feel any different with it on. It was thick and wide, yet rather plain looking. The only thing out of the ordinary was the fact that it glowed with a soft, white light, but then so did everything else in the room.

"Are you going to sit down?" Jazmin asked, smiling at Samantha's look of wonder.

"Oh . . . yes."

Jazmin passed Samantha a plate as she pulled herself up to the table.

"Salad with ranch dressing in the bowl," Evenina said very clearly.

Instantly, the bowl was packed with greens, sprinkled with ranch dressing. Small radishes, peppers, and cauliflower were mixed in, giving the salad a rather appealing look.

Evenina grinned broadly. "That's all you have to do. Beef enchiladas, beans, and wild rice."

Just as the food had appeared in the bowl, it did so on her plate, and exactly like she had said. The food was steaming hot and she blew on it, while picking up her mug.

"And lastly," she said with relish, "root beer."

Her mug was frothing with root beer in an instant.

Samantha was stunned. Could it be that you actually dreamed up what you wanted, and it just appeared? And it was real food? She looked at Jazmin, who gave a nod.

"Just say what you want," she urged. "Go on."

Samantha swallowed and cleared her throat. Then she laughed. "It's funny, I don't know what I want."

"It takes a while to remember what kind of food you like."

"Okay —" Samantha rubbed her hands together. "Here goes. In the bowl — twenty-four-hour salad."

The salad, a mixture of peas, lettuce, cheese, bacon, water chestnuts, and a host of other vegetables, filled the bowl.

"Twenty-four-hour what?" Evenina nearly choked.

"It's a type of salad my mom makes. It's really good."

"Well, don't stop there," Jazmin said, motioning with her hand. "Go for your plate now."

"Right . . . okay . . . top sirloin steak, medium rare, and a baked potato — no — wait — steak fries with ketchup."

Her plate instantly filled with her requests.

"This is too much," she laughed, turning her head and seeing Fox across the room. It was obvious he had been watching her because he smiled and gave her the thumbs-up sign. She managed to get a glimpse of his plate, which was filled with barbecued ribs drenched in sauce, some of which had found its way onto the front of his shirt.

"Pizza . . . Hawaiian," Jazmin offered.

Samantha watched as the pizza appeared on Jazmin's plate.

"Whoops — forgot. Sliced, please."

The pizza sliced itself.

"Pizza — she has pizza at least three times a week," Evenina grunted before taking a drink of root beer.

Seeing this reminded Samantha that she needed a beverage as well. "Mello Yello," she said, and the mug filled with the citrus soda, bubbling over the rim.

"What a meal," Jazmin said, looking at Samantha's combination.

For the next few minutes, they said very little and ate very much. By the time they were finished, their plates were empty and their stomachs full.

Samantha took a moment to look around at the other people seated in the room. There were probably thirty people, just about as many boys as girls and all of them, Samantha figured without the help of her Vest, were teenagers. The only one who obviously wasn't in his teens was a boy seated by himself in the middle of the room. He was eating what looked like pudding, reading intensely in a thick book that surprisingly wasn't glowing white.

Using her Vest, Samantha concentrated on him. Jazmin watched and seemed to know what Samantha was doing because before Samantha had any information, Jazmin spoke.

"His name's Seth."

"Seth?"

"Yeah. He's eight. He got his power from a Chest last year."

"And his power is the ability . . . to . . . hear . . ." Samantha was gathering the information from her Vest, ". . . which means he can hear things from great distances, and he can probably hear me right —"

The little boy turned his head and smiled gently. *I can hear you*, he mouthed.

Samantha grinned. "I like your power."

He mouthed *thank you* and then went back to his book. Samantha turned her attention to others. There were four boys seated along one of the other windows. The brown-haired boy was Tom Kitts with the Gift of Time. Samantha focused on him for a moment. . . . time . . . what did that mean?

Then it came to her. He has the ability to slow down time.

"Interesting," she whispered to herself before continuing her scan.

Seated next to Tom was Mark Deppice. He had the power to read people's thoughts. Across the table, the red-haired, freckle-faced boy was Dean Palmesad with the power to change the shape of objects. Then there was Marcus Azurdia — an older, dark-haired, mustached teenager with the Gift of Wisdom.

"You're learning about each one of them, aren't you?" asked Evenina.

Samantha nodded.

"The best power, in my opinion," Evenina added brightly, "is Charlie Cathedral's. He's over there eating by himself. He's a bit of a loner, but he has the power to shield."

"Shield?" Samantha asked, deciding not to use her Vest but rather let Evenina explain.

"He can shield himself and others from anything. He creates a shield that nothing can penetrate."

"No, no, that's not the best power," Jazmin cut in. "Over there, by Fox's table. The second boy to the right, see him?"

Samantha saw the boy. He was blond-haired with crystal-blue eyes and thin lips. He was laughing with his friends, exposing his full set of braces.

"That's Valerio. He's really nice, and he has the power to control nature."

"What do you mean?" asked Samantha curiously.

"He can control nature; stuff like the weather, rivers, lakes, trees — just about anything and everything outdoors."

Evenina coughed. "Jazmin only says he has the best power because she likes him."

"Oh, be quiet!" Jazmin snapped. "And who do you like? Huh? Should I tell her, or maybe her Vest should."

Evenina went red in the cheeks. "Pete," she whispered.

"Oh, really?" Samantha smiled, but it was a weak effort. She herself had been rather taken by Pete earlier.

"Got any favorites?" Jazmin asked before going on to say, "Clean up."

Samantha shook her head as all of the plates and bowls suddenly disappeared.

"It's great. No dishes to do, either," Jazmin smiled.

As quickly as the plates disappeared, a new set of five materialized in the center, along with bowls, mugs, and more utensils.

"Dessert," said Evenina quickly. "One hot slice of home-made apple pie and one scoop of vanilla ice cream on top."

In a brief second, Evenina was looking at her request. The other girls watched as Evenina jammed her fork in and took a bite.

"Homemade apple pie and a scoop of vanilla ice cream," said Jazmin.

"That looks so good." Samantha rubbed her hands together. "I'll have the same. A piece of homemade apple pie and one scoop of ice cream, please."

She was about to take a bite of her newly formed dessert when a boy slid up to the table, grabbed a chair and sat in it backwards.

"Jaz, who do you play first?"

Jazmin swallowed before replying. "Don't know. We haven't checked. You?"

"Mathias, Garret, and Charlie."

"Good luck," she said kindly.

"Just think of it — playing for a second power." The boy took a long, deep breath.

"This is what I've wanted ever since I became a Brilliant. To have two powers."

"I'd hate to feel the fatigue on that," Evenina said.

The boy ignored Evenina's comment. "Did you hear? Defense needs another player because one of his got sick."

Samantha concentrated on the boy with her Vest. His name was Jacob Alloy, fourteen years old.

"Septimus . . . Defense?" Jazmin sat up straight. "I thought Brent and Walden were his partners."

"Yeah, but I guess Walden got sick, and they need to find someone to fill in for him. It's going to be tough, though. He played on Septimus' team five years ago at the last tournament and almost won."

"I remember," Jazmin said, reflecting back. "That's when team . . ."

But Jazmin didn't finish. In fact, when *he* entered, the entire Banquet Hall went silent as everyone stopped talking, turning their collective heads toward him.

The first thing Samantha noticed about the man was his impressive physique. He stood six-foot-seven and was very well built. Muscles bulged out of his short sleeves, exposing large veins in his biceps and massive forearms. He had long, silver hair that hung over his ears in waves, stopping just below his shoulders. He stopped and surveyed the room. Slowly, everyone went back to their meals as he stood silent — searching.

Samantha couldn't help but analyze him further with her Vest. Concentrating, his name came to her immediately.

Septimus Flynn: the seventh and last child to be born in his family, thus his name. Septimus — Latin for seven.

She concentrated harder.

Thirty-five years old — had his Vest for nearly twenty years. Trained in the martial arts.

Septimus turned his head in Samantha's direction and began walking toward her table. She stared, mesmerized.

Was married at twenty-three and had a son two years later. Son's name was Daniel.

He drew nearer.

His wife and son were — killed by Melt while he was away on a mission for the Maker.

Samantha was sick to her stomach. She wished she hadn't used her power to learn about this man. But the information kept coming.

People believe him to be one of the most powerful Brilliants still alive. And he has the Gift . . . of . . .

Samantha was straining. Septimus was pulling up a chair.

The Gift of Defense.

"Samantha Banks," he spoke quietly, without emotion.

"Yes," Samantha said timidly.

The large man looked Samantha over slowly and then said, "Stand up."

"What?"

"Stand up," he said, more like an order.

Samantha jumped to her feet.

He looked her over and nodded approvingly.

"Can I sit down now?"

He motioned for her to sit.

"Did my homework on you," he said, this time with a low, powerful voice. "Quite an athlete you are."

"Athlete?"

"Yes. Play a lot of sports, don't you?"

"Yes."

"I need you to be my eyes."

When Septimus said this, Jacob nearly fell off his chair.

"What?" Samantha was utterly confused. He obviously wasn't blind. How was she to be his eyes?

"I figure you have the Vest of Knowledge and can learn just about anything about everything. I assume you've learned something about me already?"

Samantha nodded.

"What's my name?"

"Septimus Flynn."

"What do some people call me?"

"Defense."

"I assume you know things about me that will stay where you found them — in my mind and now yours."

Samantha nodded again.

"Then I won't explain what I mean when I say I need your eyes. The tournament is on Saturday, so you don't have a lot of time. I'll hold a practice session tomorrow. Check the message screen in your room to find out the time, and don't be late."

At this, Jacob actually fell off his chair. Septimus didn't give the boy so much as a glance, only got up, turned, and walked out of the room.

"Can you believe it?" Evenina said, astonished. "He asked you! You're to be his eyes."

Jacob managed to pick himself up off the floor.

"I can't believe it. Why didn't he ask me? He could've asked me. I'd play for him."

"You're already on a team," Jazmin reminded Jacob. "Samantha isn't."

"Jazmin, Samantha doesn't even know how to play!" Evenina pointed out.

"Play what?"

"CTF."

"What's CTF?"

"Capture the Flag," Evenina responded.

"I know how to play Capture the Flag. Played it lots of times at school."

Everyone laughed except Samantha.

"Not like this," Evenina said, waving her hand. "This is a game like you've never played before. Trust us."

"Yeah." Jacob leaned forward on his chair, his face close to Samantha's and very serious. "This game is played in an enclosed Field."

"A Field?"

"That's right, but I'm not talking about some sort of football field or something. This game is played on a Field with conditions you've never experienced before. On one side is the green team and the red team is on the other side. At each end is a flag. Your job is to get the other team's flag while defending your own."

Jacob was becoming more animated.

"The team that captures the other team's flag first, and is able to successfully defend their own, advances to the next round, and the losing team is out."

"Well then, I'll do fine. I told you, I've played this before."

Jacob went on. "Your base at the end of the Field is a three-leveled, open-faced tower. Your flag is located on the second level. The same is true with the other flag in the other tower. In between the green and red towers is a hilly Field that you must make your way across to get to the other team's base."

Jacob took a breath, and Jazmin took over.

"It sounds like you're on Defense's team now. Each team is made up of three Brilliants. Everything, from this game to our missions are always done in threes — three Vests. Three or more Vests are always to be together when on a mission. The same is true with CTF."

Jacob joined back in.

"But once you step onto the Field, your Gift is useless. You won't have the power of knowledge when you step on. You won't have any power until you're assigned one."

"What do you mean, assigned one?" Samantha frowned.

"Before the match begins, your team will meet at the base of your tower. There, you will see three Chests. One will be marked EYES. One will be marked FLIGHT, and one won't be marked at all.

"The one that's marked, EYES, will give you the Gift to see from great distances and the ability to zoom in and out like a telescope. If you open the one marked FLIGHT, you'll have the power to fly. And if you open the one that looks like the ghost of a Chest, you'll have the power of invisibility."

"For good?" Samantha gasped.

"No, just for that game."

"So, each team has three players," Samantha said, counting on her fingers. "One has the power to see and zoom in. One has invisibility, and the other has the ability to fly."

"Right." Jacob slapped his hands together. "Got it."

"And Septimus wants me to be his eyes, so he wants me to be the one who chooses the Chest marked EYES, right?"

"I would assume," Evenina said, taking the last bite of her apple pie.

"So, where's the playing Field?"

"An announcement will be given," Jazmin said. "Then you'll be taken there. We'll be watching from the stands."

"Oh my," Samantha said, nervously.

"Floating rows of seats are set up all around the Field so that we can all watch."

"But that's not everything." Jacob was in his element. It was obvious he loved the game. "As soon as you step onto the Field, the players are given a special ability — to shoot balls of light from their hands."

Samantha shook her head. Maybe she should ask her Vest because Jacob was confusing her. "What?"

"You can form balls of light in your hands and shoot them at the other team. All you have to do is aim your hand and think about the balls of light, and they'll come out."

"Why?"

"Because if you hit any of the other team's players with the balls of light, it sends them back to their base at the bottom level."

"Understand?" Jazmin asked.

"Yes, I think so. Is that it?"

"No. We've got to talk about the Rocket Anchor and the Speed Skates," Jacob continued, speaking even faster now, which Samantha was finding more difficult to comprehend.

"The Speed Skates and Rocket Anchor are objects that can be found anywhere on the Field. If you happen to find one, you're in luck because they'll help you get to the other side more quickly. The hardest thing is getting across the Field to the other team's tower. That's why the Speed Skates are so cool. If you find them, put them on, and you'll have the ability to skate across the Field in no time, while hovering above the ground.

"The Rocket Anchor is different. It's like a miniature crossbow that shoots out a small anchor. As the anchor goes flying, a trail of light will come from it, like the tail of a comet. Once the anchor hits, either on the ground or on the other team's tower wall, it will pull you to it in breakneck speed, even faster than the Speed Skates."

Samantha was trying to absorb it all. Two towers, one of them at one end of a Field, the other on the opposite end. The goal: to get the other team's flag. In order to do that, cross the Field, get to the middle level of the tower, steal the flag, and bring it back to her own base, all without getting hit by a ball of light.

"But what happens if I have the flag and I'm hit with a ball of light?" she asked.

"You'll be transported back to your tower, and the other team's flag will be returned to the original tower. Getting hit with a ball of light when you're carrying the flag is not what you want to have happen," Jacob explained.

"So, I'd have to go back and get it again?"

"Yep."

"Now, let's go over some strategies," Jacob suggested, still full of energy.

"Isn't it possible that I might play against you?" asked Samantha.

"Yeah, but I want you to know some of the strategies so that you're not totally lost."

"I think I've had enough for today," Samantha said, getting up from the table. She had hardly touched her apple pie. Jazmin and Evenina stood up with her.

"Talk to you later about it then." Jacob smiled. "What an opportunity. You are so lucky to be playing with Septimus. Good luck."

THE BANKS

The three girls hadn't gone far when around the corner came the medium-framed man known to everyone in the Lighthouse as the Maker. He was six feet tall and wore a plain pair of blue jeans and a black, short-sleeve shirt, almost the same color as his skin. His eyes were a deep brown, and as Samantha looked into them, she couldn't help but think that they sparkled somehow.

His face wore the look of an older man, probably in his seventies, but his body looked remarkably young and fit. He was thin and in shape with toned, muscular arms. He had very little hair left, and what was still there was short gray fuzz.

"How was dinner?" he asked in a kind, grandfatherly voice.

"Great, as always," Jazmin said, smiling.

"Cooked it myself," he joked. "I was hoping to catch you here. Was wondering if I might have a word with you, Samantha."

Jazmin and Evenina looked at her and smiled. "We'll see you later."

They walked out of the Banquet Hall, followed by Jacob, leaving Samantha and the old man alone. He motioned to a nearby table and slid a chair out so Samantha could sit down. "Ah, don't look surprised. Us old guys are still gentlemen."

Samantha sat down and waited for him to take a seat before asking the question.

"You're the Maker, aren't you?"

He grabbed a bowl from the middle of the table and looked at it briefly before saying, "Bread pudding in milk."

Instantly, the pudding appeared in the bowl, smothered in milk. Samantha had never seen bread pudding and, as he took a bite, thought that it looked rather disgusting.

"Sorry — been having a craving all day for this."

"How did you do that without using a Belt?" asked Samantha.

"Well, I am the Maker — at least that's what I'm called. No one calls me by my actual name anymore."

"What is your actual name?"

"Surely that Vest of yours can tell you."

"Your name is Carl Finch," Samantha said evenly.

"Very good. Is that all it's telling you?"

Samantha was silent a moment. "You're seventy-three years old. You have five children and fourteen grandchildren. You've had your Vest for nearly sixty years."

"And what does my Vest allow me to do?" he asked through a mouthful of pudding.

"It allows you to make things — objects."

The Maker stopped chewing and looked at her curiously. "And —"

"And . . . you don't like your power." Samantha frowned.

"Very good, young Samantha."

"Why don't you like your power? The ability to make things, almost anything . . . how could you not like that?"

The Maker took one last bite and then wiped his mouth with a napkin before answering. "I would dare say that the power I have is one of the greatest of all the Vests. The Gift to make an object comes with a price and a responsibility. Regrettably, in my youth, I forgot that. Made a lot of mistakes — mistakes that I have to live with. No, if I'd had a choice, I would've wanted your power."

"Mine?"

"Yes, the Gift of Knowledge. It is the greatest power."

"It's not as good as your think. A lot of times I can't get an answer I need."

"You haven't trained your mind enough yet. That will come

with time and practice."

Samantha nodded slowly.

"What did you notice when you walked into the Banquet Hall today?"

"I noticed many things." Samantha shrugged her shoulders.

"Like?"

"Kids of all ages eating whatever they could think of. I noticed the moon, the earth." She pointed toward them through the window. "The size of the room — the round tables —"

"But what was missing?"

"Missing?"

"Yes, something was missing, wasn't it? What was it?"

Samantha's eyes went from side to side for a few moments as she probed her memory using her Vest. "There weren't any . . . adults," she said slowly.

"Except for Septimus, all of the people you saw in the hall were kids — no one older than seventeen. Now," the Maker leaned forward so that his elbows were resting on the table, "when you faced the three Dark Vests in the barn last year, what were they?"

"How did you know . . ." Samantha paused. "They were adults,"

"Why is that?"

"I . . . I don't know."

"Why would most of the Brilliants be children and most of the Dark Vests adults?"

"Because children are nicer than adults?"

The Maker laughed. "Are they? It's been my experience that children can be just as mean, if not meaner than adults."

"I don't know, sir," Samantha said.

"Children believe more easily than adults. If I tell a child that I have a special power, an ability to make almost anything I can think of, he doesn't question it. He simply believes it. But if I tell an adult that, the first thought that comes to his mind is that I'm crazy because no one has ever heard of such a preposterous thing. So, most of the Brilliants are young because they believe so easily; but once you start to doubt, once you start to not believe that the Vests are real — that's when you'll lose your Gift."

"Lose it forever?"

"Forever. But you see, most of the Dark Vests are adults. They do believe in their power because they use it for their own purposes — to serve themselves and their leader. Just like the three you faced in the barn that day. All of them believed in their powers and so, as adults, they still possessed them. It was only last month that we lost a Brilliant because she failed to believe in the Gift she had been given."

"How could she not believe? Look at this place! How could someone not believe?"

"You say that now, but rest assured you'll have days when you doubt your Gift."

"No, I won't."

The Maker smiled, exposing his full set of teeth. "I see you doing great things, Samantha. But now," he clasped his hands together, "to the business at hand. It's time you told your mom and dad about your power."

Samantha raised her eyebrows. "Excuse me?"

"You will not be able to complete your missions and duties here without them knowing and giving their permission."

The Maker stood up. "Clean up," and the dirty bowl vanished.

"But . . ." Samantha stood up. "They won't believe me."

"Probably not."

The Maker brought his wrist close to his mouth. Around it was a small, golden Bracelet that Samantha thought looked familiar to her.

"Everyone has a Bracelet," the Maker said, noticing Samantha's curious stare.

"I've noticed everyone wearing one, and last year in the barn the Envoys had them, too."

The Maker sighed deeply. "Yes, they had Bracelets as well."

"What do they do?"

"Ah, you'll find out soon enough. Jazmin," he spoke into the bracelet, "I'm still in the Banquet Hall. Please come, and bring Samantha's Bracelet.

"This is how all Brilliants communicate with each other. By bringing it up to your lips and saying the name of the person you want to speak with, you open up a channel so that person can hear you."

"So, Jazmin just heard you?"

"Yes, and not aloud. She heard my voice in her ear, like a whisper."

A sudden flash illuminated the room, and Jazmin was standing only a few feet away. In her hand was a golden Bracelet.

"You'll want to put that on," the Maker said as Jazmin handed it to Samantha. "It will also act as a teleporter back to the Lighthouse, in case you ever need to get back here. Just raise it to your mouth and say 'Lighthouse'. It will bring you back here in a few seconds no matter where you are in the world."

Samantha looked at the Bracelet as it glowed softly around her wrist. "Does it always glow like this?"

"No, only briefly. It will go away in a few seconds. Just don't ever take it off," Jazmin said.

"The three of us are going to visit Samantha's parents, and we're going to tell them about her power," the Maker said, addressing Jazmin.

"Oh." Jazmin nodded. "This is always interesting."

"You've done this before?" asked Samantha, looking at Jazmin with apprehension.

"Many times."

"In fact, after we visit with your parents, we're going to see

George's and Juan's, too," the Maker said casually.

"Where are George and Juan?" Samantha asked.

"Had a chance to talk with them not too long ago. I suspect they'll be coming to eat a little later. Lance was giving them the full tour. He tends to ramble."

Jazmin gave a nod.

"So," the Maker motioned with open palms, "you ready?"

"I think so," Samantha said meekly.

"Jazmin, shall we?"

In a flash of bright white light, the three of them were standing at Samantha's front door. The Maker stepped forward and rang the doorbell, his Vest shimmering brilliantly, as were Jazmin's and Samantha's. Loud footsteps followed, and the door opened quickly. Standing on the threshold was Samantha's father, trailed by her mother.

"Samantha? Oh, thank God!" Her father opened his arms.

Samantha stepped forward and curled into them as her mother came to their side.

"Where have you been?" her father asked sternly. "I've been worried sick. Your brothers are out looking for you. The school called, they didn't know what had happened. "

The Maker shot a quick look to Jazmin and shook his head. "We're going to need with talk to Tristen about this," he whispered. "That shouldn't have happened."

"What did you say?" Samantha's father asked roughly.

"She's been with us," the Maker said kindly.

Samantha's father frowned at the strangers. "And who are you?"

"My name's Carl, and this is Jazmin. I'm sorry it's taken so long to see you. Ah," the Maker paused awkwardly, "may we come in?"

Mr. Banks moved Samantha by the shoulders so that she stood behind him. "No, you may not come in. I want you to know the police are aware she's missing."

"She was never missing, I assure you, Mr. Banks."

"I don't know you. I've never met you!"

"I understand this is quite strange, but if you'll let me explain . . ."

"Heidi, take Samantha upstairs and then call the police!"

"Dad, no! They're my friends!"

"Go now!" her dad shouted.

Samantha's mom pulled her by the arm and dragged her upstairs.

"No. Dad! Dad! Mom, stop it! Let me go!"

"You best leave!" Mr. Banks said, pointing at the two strangers before slamming the door.

The Maker stared blankly.

"Never easy, is it?" Jazmin mumbled.

"No. Just once I wish it would be. Take us in, Jaz, and follow my lead."

"You got it."

In a flush of light, they were inside the house at the base of the stairs. Mr. Banks was halfway up when he sensed something and turned, nearly losing his balance at the sight of the strangers, now in his house.

"I locked the door!" he said angrily. "Who do you think you are?"

Samantha was arguing with her mother from one of the upstairs bedrooms as her father charged down the stairs. "Get out!" he shouted, now nose to nose with the Maker.

"Mr. Banks. I would like to explain to you . . ."

"I don't want an explanation. As far as I'm concerned, you kidnapped my daughter. I've never met you before in my life!"

"I understand you're upset, Mr. Banks, and I can sort all of this out if . . ."

Then Mr. Banks did something he shouldn't have. In his anger and confusion, he swung his fist and smashed it into the Maker's cheek. The Maker turned his head as a small trickle of blood leaked from a cut in his upper lip.

"GET OUT!" thundered Mr. Banks.

Jazmin was ready to pounce, but the Maker held out his hand. He turned his head and glared at the fuming Mr. Banks. "I'll give you that one. I probably deserved it, but if you try that again, I'll be forced to do something I really would like to avoid."

This didn't seem to deter Samantha's father. He raised his fist again, but in an instant was wrapped tightly in what looked like duct tape, from head to toe. There were only a couple of slits for his eyes, nose, ears, and mouth. The rest of his body was completely covered in gray, like some sort of taped statue.

He was saying something, but it was only muffled noise. Even though Jazmin could only see his eyes, there was a look of panic and fright in them. She had to refrain from laughing.

Samantha was still arguing with her mother when the Maker called, "Samantha, you need to come downstairs."

But he highly doubted that he'd been heard. He looked at Jazmin and then lifted Mr. Banks, hoisting him up and walking him into the living room, standing him next to the fireplace.

"Now, Mr. Banks, we're all going to have a very civilized conversation, and you're going to listen. I know you're going to listen because I'm not going to remove the tape that's binding you until I've finished talking."

The Maker sat down in a comfortable, cushioned rocking chair. "Sit down in the other chair, Jazmin, and teleport Samantha and her mother down. Put them on the couch."

Jazmin nodded, and in another explosion of light, Samantha and her mother were sitting on the couch. Mrs. Banks let out a howl that sounded like a foghorn, and even Samantha stared wide-eyed at her father who stood adjacent to the fireplace wrapped in duct tape.

"Michael . . . Michael . . ." Mrs. Banks got up and moved toward her husband.

"He's fine, Mrs. Banks. Please sit down," the Maker said kindly.

"You! You did this! I'm going to call. . . "

"You're not going to call anyone!" the Maker raised his voice, and for the first time Samantha understood why he was the leader of the Brilliants. In that voice was leadership, wisdom, and power.

"Very good. Thank you. I need you to keep quiet for the next few minutes as I explain to you what your daughter is and what kind of a power she has. Can you keep quiet or do I need to tape you up as well?"

Mrs. Banks looked bewildered, but managed to shake her head no, just as Samantha burst out laughing. This seemed to open up Jazmin because she was in hysterics moments thereafter. Even the Maker cracked a smile before he started his explanation.

For the next hour, the Maker explained everything to the Banks. He let Samantha tell them about how she, Juan, and George had gotten their Gifts in Boulder Cave and how her power worked. The Maker talked to them about the Brilliants, the Lighthouse, and the struggle against the Dark Vests. The entire time, Mrs. Banks kept silent and, of course, her husband didn't really have a choice.

"Now, Mr. Banks, if I take off the tape, I assume you'll be reasonable?"

Mr. Banks mumbled just before the Maker said, "Dissolve."

Suddenly the tape that had immobilized Mr. Banks disappeared. He looked like an artifact that had been frozen in ice a thousand years. His mouth was open so wide you could've stuffed a small lemon in it. He finally sat down on the carpeted floor, rubbing his face with the palms of his hands.

"How about a soda?" the Maker said cheerfully. "No?"

A Pepsi magically appeared in the Maker's hand. He popped it open and took three large, loud gulps, and wiped his lips with his fingers. "Anybody else?"

"I'll have a root beer," Jazmin said. In a flash of light, a cold can was in her hand.

"Pepsi, too," Samantha said. A can of Pepsi ma-terialized for her.

"Mr. Banks? Mrs. Banks?"

Neither of Samantha's parents said a word and for a long time the room was silent, except for an occasional slurp.

"Is this a dream?" Mr. Banks finally asked, very slowly.

"Not a dream, Dad," Samantha answered, setting her soda down on the coffee table. "Everything he told you is true. But if you still don't believe him, test my power. What is something that would be impossible for me to know that happened to you when you were young. Something you haven't told me."

Her father looked at her strangely.

"What about the time you snuck out at night and wrecked Grandpa's truck when you were only fourteen and driving without a license?"

"How did you . . ."

"You see, Dad? It's my Vest! I have the Vest of Knowledge. You can't see it right now because you're not a Brilliant, but be-lieve me, there is a Vest of Light wrapped around me. I've been given a power, and I want to help the rest of the Brilliants. I want to learn about their world. That's the whole reason the Maker came to see you today. You need to know, and you need to let me go with them."

Samantha was speaking confidently and her resolve and strength were not only impressing Jazmin and Carl, but her parents as well.

Mr. Banks stared down at his feet, and for a long time no one in the room spoke. Finally, he looked up, staring at Saman-tha, then moving his gaze to the Maker.

"Mister . . ."

"You can call me Carl."

"Right," Mr. Banks whispered. "Carl . . . what you're telling me . . . it sounds so unreal."

"I assure you, Mr. Banks, it is real."

Samantha's mother stood up and walked over to Samantha, embracing her.

"Everything I said is true, Mom," Samantha said reassuringly.

"I believe you," her mom whispered. "But perhaps," she turned toward Carl, "you wouldn't mind explaining it again. I don't quite fully understand everything you said. Like the Lighthouse and . . ."

"Yes," Mr. Banks nodded. "I need to hear it again because I have some questions. I mean, I have a lot of questions."

"Of course you do," the Maker said kindly. "But I don't think the girls need to stay down here for another round. Why don't the two of you go outside or . . ."

"Yeah, come up to my room," Samantha said brightly, pulling away from her mother and gesturing for Jazmin to come with her.

"Okay," Jazmin said, getting up and following Samantha.

"We'll be up in my room Mom," Samantha said.

"Fine," her mom said, watching her take Jazmin around the corner and up the stairs.

The adult voices faded away while the two girls made their way up to Samantha's room. It was decorated with posters from various music groups as well as famous actors and athletes. Jazmin looked around and stopped her gaze when she saw the large framed picture with Samantha in the middle, flanked by Juan and George. At the bottom of the picture were the words, BEST FRIENDS. Jazmin took a few steps closer and stared at the smiling faces.

"You've been friends a long time, huh?" Jazmin asked.

Samantha hopped up on the bed and sat cross-legged. "Since we were in preschool."

"Juan's cute," Jazmin said sweetly.

Samantha chuckled. "Yeah, I guess. I really don't look at him like that. He's more like a brother. When you know someone so long, it's weird to think of them as cute, you know?"

"Yeah," Jazmin agreed, sitting down on the bed. "Samantha, when you found the Chest in Boulder Cave, did you find anything else? Was there anything in the Chest when you opened it?"

Samantha looked puzzled. "No, the Chest was empty inside. Why?"

"Just curious. Forget I asked."

"No, you asked that for a reason. What is it?"

Jazmin sighed. "We're looking for something — something that was placed inside one of the Chests but we don't know who has it or where it is."

"What is it?"

"It's called the Rod of Recall."

"What's that?" Samantha frowned, not getting anything from her Vest.

"It's a light blue rod, about the size of a ruler, and was put inside one of the Chests of Light by one of the Weavers. The problem is we don't know which Chest, or if it's even been discovered yet."

"You've totally lost me, even with my Vest of Knowledge. Weavers? The Rod of Recall?"

"There is so much for you to see and learn," Jazmin started. "I don't really know where to begin."

"Start with the Weavers," Samantha suggested eagerly.

"The Weavers are Spirits. They're responsible for the creation of new Vests, and they also repair those that have been damaged. There are seven Weavers, and they are constantly weaving threads of light to make the Vests. Each Vest they make has a special and unique Gift."

"So a Weaver made my Vest?"

"Yes, they've made everyone's."

"Even the Dark Vests?" Samantha asked.

"Sure. Every Dark Vest was first a Brilliant. It isn't until they start to use their Gift in the wrong way that their Vest turns black."

"Are the Weavers in the Lighthouse?"

"No," replied Jazmin. "They live in the Garden of Light."

"Where's that?"

"Near the Lighthouse."

"What do they look like?"

"Human, but they glow with light."

"How long does it take for them to make a Vest? And what'd you mean that they repair damaged ones?" Samantha asked.

"Depends. Some Weavers take many years to complete a Vest, and when I said they can repair damaged ones, I meant when Vests are returned to them."

Samantha stretched her legs out in front of her. "How are the Vests returned?"

"I'm not sure how they actually get back to the Weavers, but they're usually Vests that were once Dark and are no longer used by the Dark Vests — like Speed, Imagination, and Strength. The Robe stripped all of their Vests, and they were returned to the Weavers for repair."

"How long does it take to repair Vests that have been changed to Dark?"

"I don't know," Jazmin answered quietly.

"And the Weavers live in the Garden of Light?"

"Right. If you go out of the Lighthouse, you'll see the Garden in the distance. It's a wonderful place. It's like a paradise — you've never seen anything like it, believe me. I'll take you to it if you want."

"Right now?"

"No, but soon."

"Can I bring George and Juan?" Samantha asked hopefully.

"Sure."

Samantha stood as another question bubbled. "Jazmin, what would happen if the Weavers were captured or destroyed?"

Jazmin shook her head. "I don't know if they can be destroyed. I suppose the Book of Light would be able to tell us."

"What's the Book of Light?"

"It's the most important book in the entire Library. It contains the complete history of how the Brilliants came to be — everything about the Robe and Xylo, not to mention how to control the Weavers and the Laxinti."

"What are Laxinti?"

"The Laxinti are like the Weavers, except they have wings and they deliver the Vests to earth in the Chests of Light. It's the Laxinti's job to place a Chest near someone or people it feels will use the Vest to help others. Obviously, though, that's not always the case, since we have the Dark Vests to deal with. The Laxinti also live in the Garden of Light when they're not delivering Chests. But during the past year, some of the Laxinti have disappeared, and we're wondering what's going on. More than likely they have been captured or killed by the Dark Vests."

"This is too much," Samantha admitted. "What a world!"

For the next hour, the girls talked about the Lighthouse, the Maker, and a host of other topics all revolving around the Brilliants' world. When the bedroom door opened, it startled them both as they watched Mr. and Mrs. Banks walk in, followed by the Maker.

"Mom . . . Dad . . . is everything all right?"

Mr. Banks smiled softly. "Yes. Carl has thoroughly explained everything and answered my questions, but I have to know that this is truly what you want, Samantha. There's danger with this, and the thought of you getting hurt . . ."

Samantha hugged her father tightly. "I'm going to be well protected, Dad. This is what I want. I want it more than anything. Plus, it's not like you're not going to see me. The Lighthouse isn't a boarding school."

Mr. Banks rubbed the top of Samantha's head. "No, but to say you're a long way away is an understatement."

Samantha giggled while her mother joined the hug.

"I promise you, Mr. Banks, I will take care of your daughter," the Maker said gently.

Samantha's father nodded.

"So, Dad, what are you going to tell the boys?" Samantha wondered about her brothers as she pulled away from the hug.

"I'll think of something. There's no need for you to worry about it."

"What about your things? You're going to need clothes," Mrs. Banks said, opening the closet.

"As you can tell, Mrs. Banks, we've already taken care of Samantha's clothes," the Maker said, responding to the empty closet. "If there's something else that you want in the Lighthouse that we didn't transport, Samantha, now's the time to get it."

"The pink elephant that Kristina bought me, next to the dresser." Samantha smiled. It looked just like the one she had won for Kristina at the fair last year.

In a flash of light, it disappeared.

Mr. Banks drew in a breath. "It's incredible what you can do, Jazmin."

Jazmin smiled broadly.

"Are you returning to the Lighthouse?" Mrs. Banks asked the Maker.

"Just Samantha. Jazmin and I are off to see George's and Juan's parents now."

Mrs. Banks sighed. "George's parents won't be too hard to convince, but Juan's . . . dear . . . if you need help convincing them . . . "

"Don't worry, Mrs. Banks. As you can tell, Jazmin and I have done this before."

"Yes, well . . . just thought I would let you know that I'm available if you need help."

"Thank you."

Mr. Banks reached out and shook the Maker's hand. "Again, sorry about the punch."

"It's okay, Mr. Banks, really. Jazmin, if you will. And by the way, Mr. Banks, you've got a good right hook."

In a flash of white light, the Maker, Jazmin, and Samantha disappeared.

THE LIBRARY

"And this is the Library," Lance said, landing softly, followed by George and Juan, who stared incredulously at the hundreds upon hundreds of shelves that floated magically, some a few feet off the ground, others twenty, thirty feet high.

"Man alive," George whispered, "this is the biggest Library I've ever seen in my life."

"Uh-huh," Juan concurred.

"How many books are in this place?" George asked, turning in a circle. Illuminated shelves with glowing books floated everywhere he looked.

"Don't know. You'd have to ask the librarian," Lance answered, motioning with his hand toward the back wall.

"What are all of these books? Are they special books about Vests and stuff?" Juan wondered.

"Very few. The majority are just like the books at most libraries, except that all of these books have a special quality to them."

"What's that?"

"As soon as you open them, you've read them," Lance said with a grin.

"Come again?" Juan was perplexed.

"As soon as you open to the first page, you've read the entire book."

"How's that possible?" George asked.

"Because of the power here in the Lighthouse. Once you open up any book, except for the Book of Light, the power of your Vest allows you to read the book in a few seconds. And when I say read, I don't really mean read every word, but it's as though someone puts the book in your mind. It's hard to explain. Let's go over to the history section and pull a book out. You'll see what I mean."

Lance walked over to the wall where a floating sign read HISTORY and reached up, pulling a thick, golden book from the shelf and handing it to Juan.

"*The Dark Shadow* by Wilson Daniels," Juan read the title slowly and then looked at Lance.

"Go ahead," said Lance reassuringly. "Open it."

Juan looked at George.

"Yeah, go ahead. Open it, Juan."

Juan put his hand on the cover and was about to turn to the first page, when a boy suddenly darted around one of the nearby shelves and snatched the book out of his hand.

"Hey," Juan shouted.

Standing next to him was a boy who looked no more than ten. His pants were far too big, and he wore a long-sleeve shirt that was three sizes too large. His hair was a black, confused mass but seemed to fit with the fiendish grin that flashed across his face.

"Mathias . . . give it back," Lance said strongly.

"*Mathias . . . Smathias . . . I'm not Mathias. You ought to know me by now, Lance. I'm much better looking.*"

"You moron," the boy said, now in a completely different tone. "We look the same."

"*Speak for yourself,*" the boy said, now in a higher, sing-songy voice.

Juan and George looked at Lance bewilderedly.

"Juan . . . George . . . meet Mathias Braxton."

"*Just Braxton for now. Thank goodness.*"

Juan and George still looked stumped.

"Mathias Braxton is a . . . a . . . well, he's two people," Lance said awkwardly.

"I am not two people," Mathias spoke, now in a normal tone. "I refuse to acknowledge that Braxton even exists. If Brax-

ton would just behave himself, though, I might just consider . .
. ."

"Forget about it, Mathias, Smathias. I don't have to listen to you."

"Mathias is the name of the boy who is . . . well, somewhat .
. . normal, and Braxton is the name of the boy who just spoke,"
Lance said, frowning. "Braxton likes to cause mischief around
the Lighthouse. Isn't that right, Braxton?"

*"Oh, tut, tut. Not little old me. Come now, I wouldn't ever think of causing
mischief."*

"But they're the same person." George gestured with his
arm.

"Same body, not the same person," Mathias was now answering.

"How long has he been like this?" Juan asked.

"Since I've known him," answered Lance, shrugging his
shoulders.

*"Not the same body . . . not the same person . . . no . . . no . . . don't confuse
. . . we're two different people, and I, according to all the chicks in this place, am
the best looking one around."*

"I've already told you," Mathias broke in, "we look the
same."

*"Are you crazy? Look the same? If I looked like you, I'd have to hide my
face in shame."*

"Ah!" Mathias shouted in frustration. "You're incorrigi-
ble."

"You're just jealous," Braxton fired back.

"That will be enough, both of you," came a sharp, yet el-
egant voice nearby. George and Juan turned and saw a young
lady walking forward, her smooth, radiant blond hair dangling
to the middle of her back. Her eyes were narrow and electric
blue and somehow, even though George and Juan couldn't explain it, they were warm and compassionate.

"This is a Library," she spoke in a whisper. "Braxton, you

know the rules for my Library. Braxton?"

"Yes . . . Alexia . . . "

"Then I expect you to keep it down. There are some Brilliants in the study booths, and I don't need them disturbed."

"Yes . . . of course."

"Forgive me. I don't remember meeting you two before. Lance, are you going to introduce us?"

"Of course. This is Juan Ramirez and George Luisi."

Alexia reached out to shake George's hand, and for a moment he felt like he needed to bow and kiss it. He managed a feeble shake instead, as did Juan.

"Nice to meet you. Welcome to the Library. I take it Lance has explained to you how it works."

"Yes," murmured Juan and George together.

"And he's explained about the fatigue after reading?" Alexia asked.

"No, hadn't gotten to that yet."

Alexia nodded. "All of the books here are for you to read and study except the Book of Light. A few have been written by Brilliants, but most are regular books you'd find in any public Library. However, you have the ability to read these books in just a few seconds and your mind will be able to absorb most, if not all that is contained within the pages. As you read a book, your mind will become fatigued, just like when you've used your Vest for a long period of time. That's your signal it's time to stop reading and take a rest. The more you read books from this Library, the more your mind will become conditioned; you'll be able to read more and more the stronger you become."

"Have you read all the books in this Library?" Juan asked.

"Indeed I have."

"No way!" said George in disbelief. "That's impossible. There are way too many books and you are only . . . "

"Seventeen," she replied.

"Is that the Gift you got from the Chest? The Gift of Reading?" wondered Juan, brushing a hand over his face.

"No. Mine is the Gift of Hope."

"Hope?"

"Hope — that warm feeling you feel right now."

Juan and George blushed slightly.

"That's hope spreading through you. That's my Gift. When you touched me, hope spread through you. It comes from my Vest. The longer I touch someone, the more hope grows inside them. As for the Library, I happen to have another ability to be able to read the books from this Library without becoming fatigued as easily as most people. That's why the Maker made me the librarian when I was twelve. They hadn't had a librarian since Bess died."

"This is insane." Juan turned and looked at George. "I thought the barn was wild with the Robe and the Dark Vests — now this Lighthouse, the food room or whatever you call it where we ate earlier tonight with those Belts, and now — a Library where you can read books in no time at all!"

"Well, you haven't seen it all yet," Lance interrupted. "There's more to show you but maybe we've had enough for today. Why don't we head back to our rooms. There'll be plenty of time to see it all."

"The Library is open all the time, and I would be glad to help you with anything you're looking for."

"How about love?" Braxton inched forward.

"Go find someone else to harass, Braxton," Alexia said sharply.

"Has Samantha been up here yet?" Juan asked, floating closer to one of the book shelves and staring at the row of books.

"Samantha — Samantha Banks?" Alexia asked politely.

"Right."

Juan took out a glowing book and stared at the title.

"I had heard that she was a Brilliant but I was not aware that she was here in the Lighthouse. Is she staying here now?"

"Yeah," Juan said and slid the book back onto the shelf.

"Then it's true," Alexia whispered, almost to herself. "She has the Gift of Knowledge?"

"Yes," George said, inching closer. "How did you know that? And what did you mean 'it's true.' What's true?"

"I'm sorry. I was just thinking aloud. I would very much like to meet her when she gets time."

George looked at Juan curiously. "Can't you tell her? You live here, too, right?"

"I don't get out of the Library often. If you do see her before I do, please tell her I wish to visit with her. Will you do that for me?"

"Sure," George said.

"I see you've met Alexia," the Maker said, walking up behind Juan and George, followed by Jazmin. "We just came back from visiting your parents."

"Lance told us that you were going to talk to them. How'd they take it?" Juan asked apprehensively.

"Not . . . bad," the Maker smiled. "At least not as bad as Samantha's parents did. Let me just say that it wasn't necessary to bind any of your parents in duct tape."

"Duct tape?" Juan snickered. "You had to bind Samantha's parents with duct tape?"

"Just her father," Jazmin noted.

George burst out laughing. "I would've loved to see Mr. Banks wrapped up in duct tape."

"Where is Samantha?" asked Juan between laughs.

"She's in her room," Jazmin replied.

"George and Juan, I want you to know that your parents have given their full permission for your training here at the Lighthouse, and the rest of your belongings have been transported to your rooms," said the Maker. "And now if that's everything, I think it's time that I retired to a nice bath and a good book."

"Maker, I was meaning to speak with you about a certain book that's been giving off a rather strong glow lately," Alexia spoke emphatically.

"I'm sure it can wait until the morning, Ms. Pearson."

"But I . . . "

"Ms. Pearson — I think you read too much. Never thought I'd say that to a teenager. I need to write that down in my memoirs." He gave a chuckle. "Good-night, all."

The old man ambled to the center and glided upward and out of sight.

"Pearson. Your last name is Pearson?" George turned and looked at the librarian.

"Yes. Alexia Pearson."

"We should go back to our rooms and get ready for bed. We all have a long day ahead of us tomorrow," Lance said, gliding toward the center.

Juan and George followed.

"That means you, too, Mathias."

"Braxton, just Braxton."

"Whatever. Get going. You coming, Jaz?" Lance asked, as he started his descent.

"No. I'm going to stay and talk with Alexia for awhile."

"See you in the morning."

"Good-night," the two girls said as the rest of them floated away.

"You've met her?" Alexia said in an excited whisper.

"Yes," Jazmin said, equally excited.

"And . . ."

"She is strong. Her will is strong."

"Just as we hoped," Alexia sighed. "Finally, after all these years, to have someone who can read the Book of Light — actually read it and not have to rely on rumors and false hopes. I feel like I should go down to her room now and drag her up here to read the Book."

"She's not ready. Today was a big enough day without doing that."

"No, you're right. All in time, but Samantha Banks, *the* Samantha Banks. It's a great day for the Brilliants."

"Yeah."

"Oh wait, I didn't tell you," Alexia said suddenly. "The Book. It's been glowing brighter the last couple of days. You've got to come look at it."

"Really? Okay."

Jazmin followed Alexia through the maze of floating shelves and down three different aisles until finally coming to a glowing door in the wall. Like most of the doors in the Lighthouse, this one didn't have a knob or a handle. Alexia stood in front of it for a moment and then passed through as if she was sucked in by a strong wind. A moment later, the door opened and Jazmin entered.

The space was small and circular. There were no windows, and the room itself was quite plain. There was one glowing ball that hovered near the ceiling, and directly below it, sitting on a glowing bookstand, was the Book of Light. The Book reminded Jazmin of an unabridged dictionary.

"You're right," Jazmin marveled. "I've never seen it glow like that before."

"Told you."

"What does that mean?" Jazmin wondered.

"Don't know. But I bet it has something to do with the fact we have a Musicular again."

"You think so?"

"I've never seen it glow like that since I've been librarian. And I've checked on it everyday I've been here. This is a good thing."

★ ★ ★

The Gold River on Vancouver Island didn't look anything like gold, so why it was called that Malavax didn't know, nor did she really care. She was going on her seventh straight day of exploring the island and was sick of it. The last of the fading sunshine disappeared, and she was now relying on the Belt of Sight wrapped around her waist. Not only did it aid her in the search for the Laxinti, it illuminated the terrain around her, making it as bright as a sunny day.

She sat on the top edge of the riverbank staring at the deep, clear water twenty feet below. She could see five large, silvery-looking fish darting back and forth across the pool occasionally. She wondered if these were what the fishermen she had encountered earlier during the day were fishing for.

She surveyed the area carefully. The chances that she would run into another human being were improbable. She was in a remote area, and she hadn't seen any activity at all during the day except for the two fishermen. She brought her wrist in front of her face and pushed the only button on the watch.

"Ivory," she spoke to the watch as a mist of gray appeared, blocking out the digital time. "Ivory — you're sure it's the Gold River on Vancouver Island? It's so remote. There's nobody around. Why would a Laxintoth choose . . ."

Ivory appeared inside the screen and looked perturbed. "I've already told you. The Gold River."

"But this river is long, and I've been searching —"

"Search some more," Ivory said indignantly.

"Can't you give me something more?" asked Malavax irritably.

"No! Now, stop bothering me!"

"Do you think . . ."

But Malavax was cut off as the watch screen went gray and the time reappeared.

"Witch," Malavax hissed.

Malavax appreciated that Xylo trusted her and assigned her

to find and capture the Laxinti, but sometimes she found the work tedious. How many times had she searched for the elusive Spirits and come away with nothing, not even a sighting. And she did seriously question if Ivory was always one hundred percent accurate.

Malavax looked down at her waist and stared at the glowing Belt for a moment before something else drew her attention. It was a gentle flapping sound — one that she immediately recognized — the hum of a Laxintoth's wings. The sound was unmistakable and judging by the volume, it was close. She kept still and silent.

Slowly and quietly, she turned around and looked forward. In front of her, about thirty feet away, was a small knoll, and on the opposite side (she was betting) was a Laxintoth placing a Chest of Light. If she was able to capture the creature, there would only be two Laxinti and two Chests remaining.

She dropped to her hands and knees and scooted forward carefully, listening hard. She knew from experience she would have one shot at capturing the Spirit. A little further she crept, almost to the crest of the small hill.

She counted down in her mind.

Three. Two. One.

Malavax stood up, a glimmering, black Vest wrapping around her upper body. Then she froze because she couldn't believe what she was seeing. Placing two Chests of Light on the ground were two Laxinti. Out of all the years she had hunted them, she'd never seen two together.

She stared at their wings gently fluttering as they hovered over the old, worn-looking Chests. She raised her arms quickly and fired two bolts of black light, one from each hand, and both dark rays found their targets.

The Laxinti fell forward and skidded face first down to the bottom of the knoll. Malavax wasn't wasting time. She stepped forward and launched two more gusts of black, both of which hit the Laxintoth to her left as it lay motionless on the ground. She was about to send another volley toward the other Spirit, when a blast of white light caught her in the stomach and sent her reeling backwards. This Laxintoth was fighting back.

Malavax rolled over and stood up. One wounded Laxintoth still lay on the ground, moaning in pain, but the other one — was gone!

"You're defeated," Malavax spoke roughly, trying to conceal the pain in her stomach. "You're wounded. You can't escape. Come out and give yourself to the Dark Vests."

Malavax tried to quiet her breathing. She was listening — listening for any sound that might give her an inkling to where the Laxintoth was hiding. Even with the Belt of Sight around her waist, it could still easily hide in all the surrounding vegetation.

Malavax turned her attention to the grounded Spirit. "Where's the other?" she shouted.

The wounded Laxintoth didn't answer, and for a brief moment, her lack of attention almost cost Malavax her life. She didn't see the blast of light coming from the side but felt a searing pain in her left arm as though it was being ripped off. Another blast of light sailed over her head as she ducked, just in time. The other Laxintoth was behind her now. Malavax turned and from her left hand, a burst of black shot out, wounding the female Laxintoth in the neck. Malavax fired two more shots until the Spirit lay on the ground, shaking violently.

Malavax's arm felt as though it were dissolving. The sight of it almost made her pass out. It had shrunk and shriveled up to half its size like a dry sponge, flapping uselessly at her side. With her right hand, she supported her shriveled left wrist and brought it up to her face. The pain was too much now. She figured she had maybe a minute before she was unconscious. She pushed the button on her watch and said, "Fingust," waiting for the screen to clear up. It did, and she saw his old face looking back at her.

"Fingust," she gasped. "You . . . have . . . to . . . get Thry . . . got . . . two . . . Laxinti . . . but I'm wounded . . . need you . . . heal me . . . get here . . . get . . . here! GET HERE!"

★ ★ ★

A pleasantly soft, chiming sound echoed throughout the room and Samantha didn't have any trouble hearing it over the running water in the sink as she splashed cold water on her face. This was undoubtedly the doorbell. She turned the water off and went to the door, pushing the button in the center. The door slid open, and George and Juan entered.

"Hey," Samantha said pleasantly.

"Where have you been?" George asked, walking over to the round table and sliding a glowing chair out.

"Nice pajamas," Samantha mocked.

"Better than those pink things you got on," Juan shot back.

George nodded. "Yeah, Manthers, the pink's just a little, well, pink."

"I would prefer these to those stripes you're wearing, George."

George looked at his pajamas for a moment. "These aren't that bad."

"Uh-huh," Samantha grunted.

"So, where have you been? We didn't see you in the Banquet Hall," George said, laying down on Samantha's bed.

"I was in Evenina's room. We were talking."

"About what?" Juan inquired, looking out the window toward space.

"Just girl stuff."

"Like what?"

"Like none of your business," Samantha said, half sarcastically, half seriously.

"Have you been up to the Library or the Music Room yet?" George asked, staring at the ceiling while Samantha took a chair across from Juan at the table.

"No. Why?"

"It's awesome. You'll recognize the Music Room when you go up there, and the Library, I'm tellin' ya. That place is something else."

"What about the Banquet Hall!" Juan jumped in. "Man, what a way to eat."

"Yeah," Samantha laughed. "It must be so awesome to live up here all the time. Oh, which reminds me — the Maker and Jazmin went to talk to my parents. . . ."

"They talked to mine, too," Juan said.

"What about you, George? Did they talk to your mom and dad?" asked Samantha.

"Yeah."

"How did it go?"

"With my parents? Fine, I guess," George answered.

Samantha looked to Juan, who nodded. "Just fine."

"Well, it didn't go fine with mine."

This comment brought George up to a sitting position. "Why, what happened? Your dad freaked, didn't he?"

"Oh yeah. The Maker had to make a suit of tape to keep him from moving."

"Yeah, that's what the Maker said." Juan was hysterical. "A suit of tape?"

"Yeah, my dad didn't say much after that."

"Well, duh," Juan responded with a smile.

"But your parents finally said it was okay for you to be here in the Lighthouse?" George asked.

"Yep. They were pretty cool after the Maker explained everything."

"I wonder what my parents said," Juan reflected, looking

back out to space.

"You know, Jazmin asked me something weird," Samantha said in a more serious tone.

"What?"

"She asked me if there was anything in the Chest when we opened it up."

"There wasn't anything in it," Juan said, looking to Samantha again.

"I didn't think so," Samantha concurred.

"Why did she ask that?" Juan wondered.

"I don't know. She wouldn't tell me and neither would my Vest."

"Weird," grunted George.

"Yeah."

"Speaking of weird, what about you, Samantha?" Juan said, pointing accusingly.

"What?"

"All that stuff Lance told us about you being a Musicular."

"I have no idea what you're talking about," Samantha said defensively.

"Lance was going on about how you are a Musicular and have a special power."

"No one has told me that," Samantha replied, throwing up her hands. "I wonder if it has to do with that dream I had last year about the piano."

"I think it does," George added. "Something about you knowing how to understand music."

"But I can't . . ." Samantha broke off. Juan was pointing at the view screen on the wall. It read: ALL BRILLIANTS SHOULD BE IN THEIR ROOMS BY 9:30.

"They go to bed early around here," George said, getting up off the bed. "Come on, Juan. We gotta go."

Juan stood up. "Okay. Talk to you in the morning."

"Yeah," Samantha said, getting out of the chair. "You guys

stop by before you head up to the Banquet Hall for breakfast, and I'll go with you."

"Sounds good," Juan said as he pushed the button on the door.

"Good-night," Samantha said.

"Night," George and Juan replied.

MUSICULAR

September 18 - 4:00 a.m.

Samantha rubbed her eyes and looked at her watch. She had fallen asleep with the lights on, partly because she had been so tired and partly because she didn't know how to turn them off. There wasn't a light switch anywhere, and Jazmin and Evenina had neglected to tell her exactly how one turns off lights that float magically from the ceiling; and her Vest, surprisingly, hadn't given her anything, either.

Why she woke up at four in the morning was a mystery. Her eyes felt heavy and her lips dry from having slept with her mouth open. Her body was telling her to go back to sleep, but her mind was remarkably fresh and quite awake. She looked out the window into space. It was still hard to get used to the fact that she was orbiting earth.

She leaned over and hoisted herself to her feet. What was she going to do at four in the morning? Surely everyone was asleep. She went to the dresser and took out a fresh pair of socks, amazed that they weren't glowing since just about everything else in the room was. A pair of jeans, a short-sleeve white shirt, and her white Nikes followed.

Walking into the bathroom, she turned the faucet handle to H, and let the warm water run over her hands before splashing some on her face. In the corner of the counter, lodged up against the mirror, was a fresh toothbrush and a tube of toothpaste. She smiled. Even these items were glowing. Before going out into the hallway, she brushed her teeth and rinsed with a wide-mouthed glass that glowed with a soft white light.

She couldn't explain it (and when she asked her Vest, she didn't get an answer) but something was compelling her —

drawing her to the center. She made her way to the Fountain of Light that sparkled brightly and gazed up the mammoth middle of the structure. Everything was bright as always, even in the early morning hours. It was obvious that the Lighthouse never slept or worried about a power bill.

She pushed off the ground and felt a soft breeze against her face as she rose past the Banquet Hall. The third tier was without walls and wide open, with about a hundred chairs neatly arranged in lines of ten, facing a small stage and podium. The fourth tier, reserved for mental and physical training, was empty and quiet. Corridors branched off in every direction, and there were large, golden doors with handles shaped like Vests that glowed even brighter than any of the surrounding objects. She had the temptation to go and open one of the doors, but something was compelling her to continue on.

She soared higher until she came to the fifth tier, the Music Room. She floated a few moments before gliding in and landing softly on the ground. Everywhere she looked she saw them — glowing musical instruments floating magically over elaborately carved chairs of light.

Samantha smiled. She had been here before. This was the same room Nathaniel had taken her to in her dream a little more than a year ago. And just like in her dream, in the center of the room was the magnificent grand piano . . . Cfage.

She walked toward it, passing three floating trumpets, two hovering tympanies, and a shimmering golden violin. She stood in front of the piano admiring the shining keys, when she heard a voice from behind.

"Ah-ha! Young Samantha returns. Did I not tell you that you might visit here again someday?"

Samantha turned. Walking toward her, wearing a blue sweat suit and a sparkling Vest, was the old man she had seen in her dream, a dream she could never forget. As he came closer, she said his name. "Nathaniel."

"Yes. You remember me. Very good."

"I have been here before."

"Of course you have, although it was a much different situation." Nathaniel waved his hand in front of him. "You were under attack by those awful creatures. You were lucky you were able to hear Cfage."

He put his hand on the piano and patted it gently. "She saved you really, giving you that glowing ball of light to help you remember about your own Vest in a time of panic. Smart instrument, Cfage is."

"How did you know about the creatures?"

"Oh, just about everyone knows of your adventures."

"What is this place?" Samantha asked, surveying the massive room.

"This is where you can come to express your feelings, to communicate through music, and to listen, although hardly anyone comes up here anymore."

"Yeah, Evenina didn't take me here."

"Doesn't surprise me. None of the current Brilliants are Musicular, and only Musiculars can play these instruments. They're all very touchy about that. It's been years since someone has actually played any of them."

"I'm sure there are Brilliants who can play instruments. George played the trumpet for a few years in school." Samantha stopped herself. "Wait. George and Juan had a dream just like I did. They were taken here, but they had different people playing the piano for them. They were girls, if I remember right. Who were they? Other Brilliants?"

"No." Nathaniel smiled. "They were me."

"You?"

"Yes. I'm the Brilliant known as Feign," he said simply.

"Feign?" Samantha frowned.

"I have the ability to change into anyone I want to — in essence, I make myself into other people. Those girls were really me. I was just using my power to change my appearance and voice. That is the Gift I received from a Chest many years ago."

"How does it work?" Samantha asked, intrigued.

"Ah, watch."

Before she could say another word, the old man dissolved into a petite girl with long, jet black hair and bright green eyes. "You see," the little girl spoke in a high-pitched voice, "this is my ability. I can stay like this for quite a long time before I begin to get fatigued and must change back."

And the girl did so, growing back into the tall, strong frame of a man. "But here in the Lighthouse, we don't have to worry about fatigue. Besides, my duties here are to tend to the instruments, which really doesn't require me to use my Gift. However, as much as I would like to, I can't play any of them in this room because I'm not Musicular. But the instruments seem to like me, and I have a certain fondness for them.

"In the dreams, your friends couldn't hear what Cfage was saying because neither of them are Musicular."

"What do you mean?" Samantha asked because her Vest wasn't giving her an answer.

Nathaniel chuckled. "Musicular means that you're able to speak through and understand music. Music is a language, and all of the instruments in this room speak that language. It's a language only you can understand. Because of that, you are very important — important because through the music, you can foresee things that may happen in the future."

Samantha ran her hands through her thick, long hair. There was a long pause as Nathaniel looked at her, a look of great anticipation on his face.

"Musicular?" Samantha whispered.

"Yes," Nathaniel said excitedly. "Sit down on the bench and play Cfage."

"But I don't know how to play this instrument or any of these in here," Samantha argued.

"Yes, you do. Trust me. Sit down and play."

"But . . ."

"Sit . . . down . . ." Nathaniel said slowly and force-fully.

Samantha gradually lowered herself to the glowing bench and faced the smooth keys. She was again probing her Vest. How do I play? What are the black keys for?

"Go on. Play her."

"Nathaniel, I don't . . ."

"Play her."

Samantha thrust both hands down hard. She was going to prove to Nathaniel that she couldn't play, but just as her hands touched the keys, she felt them move and spread apart. Instead of the harsh, loud crash she had expected to make, she heard a beautiful chord echo smoothly around the room.

She turned and looked up at Nathaniel in wonder.

"Told you," he said, smiling.

Samantha lowered her hands to the keys again, and she was off. Her fingers danced and raced across the keyboard as if each one had a mind of its own. The music she was creating was melodic and soothing. As she played, her fingers glowed with a brilliant white light, just like her Vest.

Nathaniel put his hand on her shoulder, and Samantha stopped. "I should tell you a little more about this place before you become Lighted."

"Lighted?"

"That's what it's called when a Musicular becomes so emotional that it's impossible to get their attention. It was beginning to happen to you. When a Musicular is lighted, they have great power."

"How do you know?" asked Samantha breathlessly.

"Your hands," replied Nathaniel, pointing to her fingers. "They were beginning to glow."

"Yes, I noticed that."

"That's the first sign you're becoming Lighted."

"I see," Samantha said, sounding confident, while in truth she was very confused. Her Vest of Knowledge was failing to provide her with any of the information she needed.

"Each of the instruments in here is named. In fact, they named themselves. Cfage really wanted to be named Charlotte, but instruments here can only use the notes of the musical alphabet. So, all they have are A – B – C – D – E – F and G — nothing past G, of course. So instead, she named herself Cfage."

"You're serious?"

"Yes," Nathaniel answered sincerely. "She really likes it when I call her Charlotte, don't you, sweetie?"

To Samantha's surprise, the piano played a long, sustained chord.

"There, you see. Now, what I heard was a chord, but you possibly heard a word or a phonetic sound, didn't you?"

Samantha nodded pensively. "She said 'thank you.'"

"You see, you have the ability to understand."

Five rows away, a large double bass began to play by itself, a quick, deep running sound that caught both Samantha and Nathaniel's attention.

"That's Ababba," said Nathaniel. "What's he saying?"

Samantha smiled. "He says that he hopes I will play someone else besides Cfage."

Suddenly, Cfage let out a series of scales, followed by a long chord.

"What was that all about?" Nathaniel looked at Samantha curiously.

"Cfage says that he'll have to wait."

Nathaniel gave a hearty laugh. "It's been too long since I've heard them talk to one another like this. To finally hear music again! Samantha, you have the ability to play every instrument in here, and play them perfectly. I am envious."

"But I've never played the bass. Look how big it is!"

"You've probably never played the piano before either, have

you? It doesn't matter if you haven't played the instrument before." Nathaniel put his hand on Samantha's shoulder. "This is only the beginning."

Samantha looked at the piano keys again, and then let her hands and emotions go. The sound was beautiful and within a few minutes, she could hear many of the other instruments joining in. What started off as a solo was now turning into a full orchestra as strings, woodwinds, brass, and percussion all played together. Her hands glowed brilliant white and a feeling of great warmth and joy surrounded her as she played the keys with precision and perfection. Samantha closed her eyes and let the music fill her.

* * *

Samantha didn't remember at what time she actually fell asleep or even how she fell asleep. All she remembered was playing music with Cfage until everything had gone pleasantly white. It wasn't until she woke up in a fetal position, lying atop the cushioned piano bench, that she realized she had indeed fallen asleep there.

Rubbing her eyes and sitting up slowly, things came into focus. She was still in the Music Room, and the glowing, floating instruments hadn't moved. She slid her tongue over her teeth and licked her dry lips. She had slept with her mouth open again and wanted to gargle with mouthwash and brush her teeth.

As she stood, she was greeted by a pleasant melodic, "Hello."

She turned to her left, and floating a few chairs away, a violin magically played, the bow running smoothly over its strings.

"Good morning, Samantha."

She stared at the instrument.

"Good morning, Samantha," the instrument repeated.

"Good morning," she replied in a sleepy drawl. "What time is it?"

"Ten o'clock."

"Who are you?"

"I'm Feeda," the instrument played.

"Nice to meet you," Samantha said kindly, although it was tough to shake the feeling that talking to musical instruments wasn't normal. Of course, neither was having a Vest made of light that gave knowledge.

"I was wondering if you wanted to give me a try," the violin asked melodically.

Samantha was about to say that she didn't know how to play the violin when she caught herself and looked at Cfage.

"Okay," she said grinning and strode over to the golden fiddle.

"Wait," a deep voice boomed.

Samantha wheeled around to see which instrument had said that. At the base of one of the enormous windows, a tympani pounded away. "I would like to invite you to play over here. I am Gace. Please — come and have a try."

Samantha stared from the tympani to the violin.

"Oh, don't listen to him," the violin sounded. "He's just jealous that no one has played him in years."

"No one has played you in years, either," the tympani rumbled back.

"Be quiet, or you'll wake the others," hissed Feeda.

"Too late for that," came a long voice from near the center of the room. It was a trombone. "Fadag was sleeping well until you started your pounding, Gace. It would be appropriate if you took into consideration that others are trying to sleep."

There was a pause and Fadag continued. "Samantha Banks, the Musicular . . . pleasure to meet you. Fadag is truly happy. Please, sit down and play me. It would be an honor."

"NO!" came a bursting voice. It was a trumpet, two seats away from Fadag, the trombone. "I would be next, if you please. Aaad would be most pleased if you chose him. Aaad has waited too long to be played by one so fine a musician as yourself."

Samantha now was thoroughly confused and amazed at the same time. She could hear each instrument in two ways. In the background, she heard the actual notes that each was playing, and in the louder foreground she heard their words in English. Truly amazing, she thought to herself while Aaad and Fadag argued over who played louder.

"Maybe," Samantha said, holding a hand up in the air, "I will go and eat first before I actually play anyone."

The instruments stopped their chatter, and the room fell silent. She walked toward the opening in the center of the room and was about to float off when she heard a very dark, very low sound come from behind her.

"Play . . . me . . ."

She stopped and stared. Nestled along the wall, propped on a stand, was a xylophone being played magically by two golden mallets.

"Too long . . . since . . . play . . . me."

The voice speaking was dark and mysterious and over-whelmingly powerful. Samantha felt cold run through her as though ice was now replacing blood, and she suddenly wanted to play — she needed to play the instrument.

"Yes, come. Come play me, now."

Samantha moved toward the xylophone slowly.

"DO NOT PLAY HIM!" Cfage played roughly. "HE IS FOR-BIDDEN! HE IS EVIL!"

Samantha glanced at the glistening piano.

"Play . . . me . . . " the xylophone pinged.

Samantha was becoming colder, yet the yearning to play the xylophone was overtaking her.

"Play . . . me . . . Samantha."

Samantha took another step.

Cfage was raging. "DO NOT! IT IS FORBIDDEN! HE WILL CORRUPT YOU! DO NOT PLAY HIM!"

Before Samantha could get any closer, Jazmin touched her shoulder. "Finally, found you."

The cold feeling inside Samantha dissipated, along with the lust to play the xylophone.

"Are you all right? What were you doing?" Jazmin asked, looking a bit concerned.

"Umm, nothing. I . . . a . . . "

"Been looking all over for you. Didn't think you were up here but Feign was talking at breakfast, so I figured I'd look. But," Jazmin was looking her friend up and down, "you look like you've had a rough night."

"Oh, yeah," Samantha said, brushing the hair from her eyes. "I fell asleep on the piano bench."

Jazmin shook her head in disbelief. "You fell . . . asleep here in . . . the Music Room?"

"Yes."

Jazmin laughed. "Come on, let's get you some breakfast."

They walked to the edge, and just as Samantha was ready to float into the center, the xylophone struck a set of chords.

"You . . . will . . . play . . . me . . . "

A cold chill ran up Samantha's spine.

"What was that?" Jazmin said, floating into the center. "Did you understand it? What'd it say?"

"Oh, nothing," said Samantha dismissively, jumping into the center.

"I don't know if Evenina told you yesterday, but your classes begin today at noon."

"Classes? No, she didn't mention that to me. Do Juan and George know?" Samantha asked as they gradually descended.

"They should. Your first session is self-defense with Septimus. George and Juan will be in the class with you. If you had slept in your room, you would've seen the message on the view screen this morning," Jazmin said with a smile.

"Oh, okay."

"Juan and George are in the Banquet Hall. They were looking for you and said you didn't answer when they knocked on your door this morning."

"Yeah, we were going to go up to the Banquet Hall and eat together."

"Well, they're waiting."

ETHAN

Ethan hated PE. Not that he didn't like exercising and sports, but it was Mr. Redmond that made life miserable. First, the teacher thought he was God's gift to every sport on the planet. This, of course, was far from the truth; and second, he hated Ethan. Whatever Ethan did, or whenever he did it, it was always incorrect. This Friday's PE class, however, would be dramatically different from the norm. Class started the way it always did with Mr. Redmond talking about . . . himself.

"Today," Mr. Redmond began, "we will be doing individual speed tests. You will start on the black line here and go all the way to the other side of the gym, touch the wall, and come back. I will use the stopwatch to record your time."

He paused and surveyed the students.

"As you probably already know, I am rather fast — ran sprints in college . . ."

Ethan closed his eyes. He had heard this before, ever since the first day of class. How Mr. Redmond had the fastest time in his college's history — how Mr. Redmond was going to go to the Olympics but couldn't because of an ankle injury — how Mr. Redmond had been written about in *Sports Illustrated* — not that any of this was bad, but it was Mr. Redmond's smugness and I-am-the-best attitude that annoyed Ethan.

"Mr. Franklin!" Mr. Redmond blasted, knocking Ethan out of his daze. "Is my class so boring that you find the need for sleep outweighs what I'm saying? You'd be wise to listen to my accomplishments, Ethan. Very few have the talent I do when it comes to running."

Ethan whispered, "And when it comes to bragging."

Jennifer Ross, who was the closest to Ethan, covered her mouth with her hand to try and muffle a laugh.

"What was that?" Redmond snapped. "What did you say?"

"Nothing."

Mr. Redmond strode over angrily, his black hair slicked back, exposing his abnormally large forehead.

"I would like to remind you and everybody else in this class, that no one — *no one* — has ever beaten me in a sprint for as long as I've been teaching here. But, there might be some competition this year," Mr. Redmond said, changing from his angry demeanor as he turned toward Larry Shoe. "Mr. Shoe might have what it takes to outrun me. I've been working with him for sometime now, and I expect if he continues to LISTEN," Redmond turned back and glared at Ethan, "he'll have the ingredients of a great sprinter."

The students fixed their gaze on Larry who was just about the most loathed kid in the class. If Mr. Redmond was the most arrogant, Larry Shoe was right behind him. When Mr. Redmond had formed the Sprint Club, Larry had been the first and only one to sign up for the after-school class.

"How many of you would like to see us race right now?"

None of the class raised a hand. Ethan figured they were feeling the same way he did.

"Who cares," Ethan said, and this time, too loudly.

Mr. Redmond spun around and pointed. "Excuse me, Mr. Franklin — did I hear you say 'who cares'?"

Ethan felt himself go red in the face.

"Who cares, really, because it's not important, right? It's not important to you because you're slow."

Ethan felt like Redmond had just slapped him in the face. Larry giggled idiotically while the rest of the class stared at Ethan, wondering how he was going to respond.

"I'm not slow," Ethan finally said, albeit weakly.

"Oh, really? Are you fast enough to say . . . beat Larry in a sprint?"

Ethan was silent. He narrowed his eyes and focused. Within a moment, a glowing Vest of Light wrapped around his upper body. He had learned early on that other people couldn't see his Vest of Light. As many times as he had used it, either playing hide-and-go-seek with Tony Rix or running home from school, no one had ever mentioned seeing it, not even his parents.

"Well, Mr. Franklin? I asked if you can beat . . ."

"I'll beat him," Ethan said strongly.

Mr. Redmond laughed. "Really? Larry, what do you think?"

Larry smiled, exposing his yellow, not-brushed-in-a-week teeth. "He can't beat me."

"My thought as well," Mr. Redmond mocked.

Ethan stood up and pointed at Redmond, anger beginning to boil inside him. "I'll beat Larry and YOU."

Mr. Redmond was doubled over in laughter. "You? You want to race me? You think you can outrun me?"

"I know I can outrun you."

"All right then," Mr. Redmond said, striding over to Larry. "Stand up."

Larry stood.

Mr. Redmond put his hand on the boy's shoulder. "Now, let's take a poll, shall we, Larry? How many of you," Redmond now addressed the class, "think that Larry will win?"

Nobody raised a hand. Larry looked very miffed, as did Mr. Redmond.

"I see. All of you think that Ethan can beat Larry? Right? Very well. We'll do this. If Larry wins, the class runs for fifteen minutes straight."

The class erupted into disapproval, but Redmond wasn't finished and held out a hand. "Well, if Ethan wins, like all of you think, you won't have to run."

"I want to change my vote," Jake Tucker blurted out, raising his hand in the air.

"Me too," a girl next to him said hurriedly.

"Oh, no," Redmond went into his sarcastic tone. "You should have thought about that when you had the chance to vote."

"But I . . ." the girl tried to argue, but Redmond cut her off quickly.

"Now that it's settled, Larry — Ethan — on the black line. The rest of you get to the sidelines, and watch Larry's superior speed."

Ethan followed Larry and Mr. Redmond to the line while the class went to the sides.

"Spread apart from each other," Redmond said as both boys put the tips of their toes on the line.

"Good luck," Larry said mockingly. "You're gonna need it."

"Uh-huh," Ethan mumbled under a smile. Ethan knew Larry could never beat him as long as he wore his Vest. The problem was making the race look normal and real. If he put on too much speed, people would ask questions, something he wanted to avoid. He would make the race close by coming from behind.

"I will count down from three, and then you will race," Redmond said, standing between the two boys.

"Whip his butt," Ethan heard someone shout from the sidelines.

"Yeah, Ethan. C'mon. Beat him!" Jennifer shouted.

Mr. Redmond gave the class a nasty look. "On my mark — three . . . two . . . one . . . GO!"

Both boys tore ahead. Ethan held back, making sure that he was behind Larry as they sprinted toward the opposite wall. Larry touched it, and Ethan wasn't but a couple steps behind. Back toward the black line they raced — Larry expending every ounce of energy and Ethan not even breaking a sweat. Ethan accelerated past Larry at mid-court and continued through easily to the black line, winning convincingly.

Mr. Redmond stood, flabbergasted, looking at Ethan as though he had just committed a crime. The class was cheering madly, Jake Tucker shouting above the noise: "I told you he was going to win! I told you!"

"What's the matter with you, Larry!" scolded Mr. Redmond. "Ethan's one of the slowest people in this class!"

Larry was speechless, staring down at his shoes with a defeated expression. Even Ethan felt sorry for him. Mr. Redmond was taking the contest too seriously, and now it was time to rub it in his face.

"All right! All right!" Redmond shouted over the students' cheers. "That's enough."

The gym became silent as Redmond turned to Ethan. "Lucky that Larry isn't his regular self today, Mr. Franklin, or your class would be running. So it seems that I'll have to show you what a true sprinter looks like in action."

"How about a bet," Ethan said, to the shock of the class. Larry looked up and frowned, as if trying to tell Ethan that this wasn't a good idea.

Mr. Redmond's eyes flashed with delight. "Of course. Once I win, the class has to do twenty minutes of laps around the gym!"

The class erupted with protest but was quickly quieted by their teacher's raised hand.

"Fine. That's if you win. What if I win?" asked Ethan.

"But you won't win."

Ethan smiled wryly. "But if I do, how about we get to tape you up on the cafeteria wall and throw Jell-O at you during lunch, like they did with Mrs. Wilkins last year when her class reached their reading goal."

Mr. Redmond laughed. "You'd like that, wouldn't you, Franklin? To be able to throw Jell-O at me."

"He's not the only one," shouted Jake. "You can do it, Ethan. You can beat him. He's an old man."

Mr. Redmond turned and shot a look of venom at Jake. "I'm thirty-two years old, Tucker. And you'd better watch it, or you're going to be doing laps all week if you don't shut that mouth of yours."

Jake fell silent.

"So, we have a deal?" Ethan asked.

"Fine. Whatever," Mr. Redmond said, waving his hand nonchalantly. "Get ready."

Ethan stepped up to the black line. Redmond did the same.

"On my count. Three, two, one — GO!"

There was no holding back this time. Ethan was not only going to embarrass Mr. Redmond in front of forty-two students, he was going to be the first one to hurl Jell-O at the pompous instructor. By the time Ethan had sprinted down and touched the wall, Mr. Redmond was ten feet behind. Ethan poured on the speed and was standing on the black line, finished, before Redmond had even made it back to the half-court line.

"C'mon, you can do it!" Ethan teased as the crowd of amazed kids went wild on the sidelines.

"Redmond! See you at lunch, Redmond!" sang Jake as their PE teacher finally finished.

Redmond looked as though he had lost something precious. "I . . . I . . ." he stammered.

"Jell-O, Redmond, JELL-O!" Jake shouted in elation.

★ ★ ★

"I've already told the both of you," Xylo said impatiently from where he sat behind a large rectangular desk. "I'm not concerned with Samantha, and that's not why I called you here."

"Yes, but Xylo, I have seen . . ." Ivory tried to interject.

"I know," Xylo said patiently. "You and Melt already expressed your concern over the girl. I do not see her as a threat, Ivory. And let's be honest, shall we? Your Gift isn't exactly always one hundred percent accurate, is it?"

"No, sir, but . . ."

"In fact, Ivory, you're lucky to get fifty percent of your predictions right."

Ivory opened her mouth to say something but decided against it. As much as she hated to admit it, Xylo was right. Her predictions were not very accurate, and it had cost some Dark Vests their lives.

"I called you both here because I have some very interesting news."

"Yes?" Melt said, stepping forward.

Xylo leaned forward over the table. "We have a Musicular."

Ivory and Melt looked at each other with disbelief.

"Sir? You're sure?"

"Yes, Melt. I contacted her yesterday."

"Who is it?" Ivory asked.

"It's Samantha."

"Samantha?" Ivory looked stunned.

"You see, Ivory, why I'm not concerned? I'm going to use her to form the bridge."

"But, sir, she is strong-willed," Ivory protested.

"NOT AS STRONG-WILLED AS I!" Xylo shouted, his temper bubbling from Ivory's lack of faith. "Believe me, Ivory. I will bridge with Samantha, and then it's only a matter of time . . . a very short time."

★ ★ ★

"You're here to be trained in hand-to-hand combat," Septimus said, his hands clenched together. "All of the Brilliants have been trained in the martial arts. You need to know how to defend yourself if you encounter a Dark Vest."

Juan, George, and Samantha stared at the man nervously. The room they were in was completely padded, from floor to wall to roof. Balls of light floated from the twenty-foot ceilings and gave off a brilliant glow that illuminated the room with magnificent shades of gold.

This was just one of many rooms on the fourth floor of the Lighthouse, the floor reserved for the physical and mental training of the Brilliants.

"The first thing you'll learn today is a basic block. You never know when a Dark Vest, or someone else for that matter, is going to strike you, either with a fist or another object. What will you do if someone attempts to hit you like this?"

Septimus stepped forward, swinging his arm toward Samantha's head. Instinctively and inexplicably, she brought her forearm up and blocked the attack. The move shocked her. It shocked Juan and George, too, and took Septimus by complete surprise. Her Vest of Knowledge was working. She already knew how to defend herself. She knew the attacks and the defenses . . . she knew.

Septimus took a step back. "Impressive. Using your Vest, are you? Let's see how you do with a more advanced attack."

Septimus charged Samantha with a barrage of high-flying kicks. Juan and George stood awestruck as Samantha held her ground and ducked easily out of the way.

"Nice," he said, sliding toward her and trying to kick her feet out from under her.

Samantha darted to her right and flipped over him with ease. Septimus turned and fired a hard right hook at her head. She blocked it easily with her left arm and then jumped into the air, bringing her foot around and slamming the side of his cheek. This move took him by surprise, and Samantha didn't wait. She gave him two quick fists to the chest. She raised her hand to hit him a third time, but felt a sharp pain in her abdomen as he planted a solid fist into her belly. The force knocked her to the ground and left her gasping for air.

"The Vest of Knowledge," Septimus said, visibly impressed, as he stood over her while she caught her breath. "Not bad, Banks. Your Gift will come in very handy."

Samantha coughed and nodded at the same time.

"Hey, you didn't have to hit her so hard!" George said angrily, stepping forward.

"You okay, Manthers?" Juan asked, kneeling next to her.

Samantha nodded again. "Fine. Wasn't ready for that move."

"Exactly," Septimus said, lending her his hand. "Come on, get up. You always have to be ready — never relax. The moment you do, the more time your enemy has to attack you. You may have knowledge, Samantha, but you need experience in battle. The only way to get that is to simulate battle here in this room or experience the real thing."

Samantha rubbed her stomach. "It hurts."

"Always be ready — always be prepared," Septimus said evenly. "Juan, I will work with you over here, and George, you will work with Samantha."

"You want me to show him the basics? Positioning, stance . . ." Samantha asked in a serious tone.

"Yes, start there. I'll do the same. We have roughly two hours for our first session. It's a good thing you arrived early and stretched. All of you will be sore because you'll be using muscles you never even knew you had."

For the next hour and a half, Septimus and Samantha showed Juan and George some of the basics, the fundamentals of karate. The boys were quick learners, and Samantha could tell that Septimus was very pleased with their progress. As the last hour of practice was ending, Septimus sat the three Brilliants down against a wall.

"These rooms are simulation rooms, which means this is where you practice. You can practice any time, by yourself or with someone else, as long as the room isn't being used. These simulation rooms have a special attribute. Now, I don't want you to panic when he comes in."

"When who comes in?" Juan asked, curiously.

In a flash of white light, a man suddenly stood in the opposite corner of the room. He was dressed in black, and a shimmering Dark Vest enveloped his upper body. George was about to stand up, but Septimus put out his hand.

"Remember, these are simulation rooms. He is a simulation. He's not real."

"Who is he?" George asked, pointing.

Septimus turned and stared seriously at the man. "That is my enemy. That is the man that killed my family."

"That's Melt," Samantha whispered.

Septimus turned his head toward her. "That's right, Samantha. That's Melt, and someday I won't fight the simulation. Someday, I'm going to meet him, the *real* him, and . . ."

"And?" Samantha said, her eyebrows raised.

But Septimus didn't answer because a bright light emerged over his head, and then formed into the shape of the glowing letter M. He looked above and nodded, obviously knowing what the signal meant.

"The Maker's calling a meeting. Practice is over for now. You need to go and get changed and meet up in the briefing center as soon as possible. We'll continue class on Monday."

By the time Samantha, Juan, and George floated up to the briefing center, nearly half of the hundred, white glowing chairs were filled with Brilliants. The Maker stood on the small stage behind a podium and grinned when he saw Samantha, George, and Juan float in and take seats in the back row.

"Sorry to interrupt your afternoon classes, everyone. Thank

you for getting here so quickly. We have learned that another Gift has been given, and due to the fact that many Brilliants are missing," the Maker paused painfully, "we are taking some new steps in ensuring the safety of all new Brilliants. Three of you will serve as Envoys and will be leaving shortly. Sarah . . ."

The Maker pointed to the front row and a tall, black girl stood and faced the audience. "His name is Ethan Franklin. He's fourteen and lives in Washington state," she said evenly.

"What's his Gift?" asked Pete Harris, sitting in the third row.

"Speed," Sarah answered.

Whispers immediately broke out. Juan and George exchanged we-remember-Speed glances while Samantha used her Vest to find out more about Sarah — Gift of Location — able to find people and things, no matter where they are.

The Maker raised his hand, and it was again quiet. "To date, forty-seven Brilliants are missing, either through disbelief or perhaps they've been captured or . . . or even killed. That's almost half of us.

"Feign, Jazmin, and Samantha — you will be his Envoys."

Samantha's stomach gave a lurch. Did the Maker just call her name?

She looked at Juan and George, who stared at her nervously.

"I will meet with the three of you after this meeting. Is there anything anybody would like to share?" the Maker asked, scanning the faces in front of him. "Very good then. Afternoon classes will begin in thirty minutes. Dismissed."

The room was filled with chatter as Samantha, George, and Juan rose from their seats. "I haven't met most of these people," George whispered.

"Me either. And there are more that aren't even here," Juan marveled. "I'm never going to know everyone's name."

Jazmin walked toward them, trailed by Evenina. "Congratulations, Samantha. It's an honor to be an Envoy."

Samantha tried to smile and look pleased, but inside, her stomach was hurting almost as bad as when Septimus had punched her.

"What exactly does an Envoy do?" George wondered aloud.

"An Envoy is a representative that goes to greet new Brilliants, and in some cases, escort them to the Lighthouse," Jazmin answered.

"Like you did with us?" said Juan, pointing at Jazmin.

"Right."

"And the three boys that were killed in the barn — they were Envoys, too, weren't they?"

"Julian, Luis, and Jannick," Evenina said somberly. "Yes, they were Envoys."

The Maker walked down the aisle, Septimus and Sarah at his side. "Septimus tells me you already know how to take care of yourself."

Samantha smiled. "I'm learning."

"Excellent. That's one less thing for this old man to worry about. Hope you're not too nervous about your first real assignment."

"No, sir," Samantha answered bravely.

"Good. I know that you're new here, Samantha, and that you don't fully understand everything, but your Gift is going to be extremely useful in times like these. That's the reason I'm sending you," the Maker said seriously before turning to Jazmin. "George and Juan, you'll have to excuse us. Jazmin, if you will —"

In a blast of light, Samantha was transported to a small circular room with gargantuan rectangular windows overlooking space. In the room with her stood Jazmin, Sarah, and the Maker.

"Jazmin, we need Nathaniel. Can you get him here,

please?"

Jazmin nodded. In a flash of light, Nathaniel was standing in the middle of the room, looking perplexed. "I hate it when you do that, Jazmin. A little warning would be nice from time to time," Nathaniel said jokingly.

Jazmin smiled.

"Honestly," Nathaniel said, donning his Vest. "I suppose I ought to be used to it by now."

"Nathaniel, I've chosen you to go along as an Envoy," the Maker said.

"Oh," Nathaniel said, nodding. "We have a new Brilliant?"

"Yes, Speed."

"Speed? Wasn't that a Dark Vest?"

"Yes."

"So the Weavers are working fast. That's a quick repair."

"Very quick," the Maker concurred.

"Is it a boy or a girl?"

"Boy," Sarah replied.

"Why don't you all take a seat, everyone." The Maker motioned to the large, cushioned, reclining chairs in the middle of the room, each glowing with a white hue. Samantha sat down and knew immediately that this was the Maker's private room. It was about twice the size of her quarters down on the first floor and had all the essentials — a double bed, a sink, towels, and an enormous, beautifully carved wooden desk — the only object in the room that didn't glow.

"Samantha, have you met Sarah?" the Maker asked.

"No," Samantha replied, smiling at Sarah, who smiled back. "Hi."

"Nice to meet you."

"Sarah has told Jazmin where you'll find Ethan, our new Brilliant. Once you get to him, you need to bring him back here to my quarters."

Everyone nodded.

"I wonder who I should go as," Nathaniel said in a high voice. "I could go as you," he said, pointing at Samantha.

Samantha watched as his body and face changed shape. His hair grew long and brown and within a few seconds, he looked like Samantha's twin.

"I could go as Samantha Banks," he said, now in Samantha's voice.

Samantha gaped at him. "Amazing!"

"Yes," he said, changing once again — this time into Jazmin. "Or perhaps I could be Jazmin."

"You're not nice enough to be me," Jazmin teased as he turned back into himself.

"I guess I'll go as myself . . . at least for now."

The Maker laughed. "As many times as I've seen you do that, it still amazes me."

"Thank you," Nathaniel smiled confidently.

"Good luck, all of you. Chances are the Dark Vests already know about Ethan as well, so be wary."

* * *

"You're sure it's down this road?" the eighteen-year-old woman known as Sickle asked.

"Yes, that was what Thry told me," the older man said, wiping sweat from his forehead. The sun was blistering.

"Well, how does Thry know?" the teenager wondered, standing on the sidewalk, scanning the street for oncoming cars.

"Ivory told her."

"Ah, Kelvin — just because Ivory told her doesn't mean anything. Thry forgets half the stuff you tell her anyway."

"Well, we're about to find out," Kelvin said, pointing down the street. "Here it comes."

Kelvin and Sickle stood side by side as the yellow bus pulled up gradually until finally coming to a stop. The red stop sign swung out just as the doors opened and two students walked off.

Both Dark Vests looked at the kids hard before turning their attention to the side of the bus, which read in bold, black letters: Sammamish Middle School - Bus 8.

"That's the bus," Kelvin said, stepping forward.

Sickle moved quickly toward the open doors and held them as Kelvin boarded.

"Shut the bus down," Kelvin shouted forcefully while Sickle followed, pulling the bus doors shut behind her.

Fifty-five-year-old Edward Pastura couldn't see the dark, glimmering Vest that surrounded Kelvin's body, but he knew by the man's expression that he, along with the students on the bus, were in danger.

"I said SHUT THE BUS DOWN"

The old man didn't know what to do. A part of him wanted to jump out of his seat and tackle the strangers, but there were two of them and only one of him. There was no way he could take them both. And there wasn't any way of reaching the cellular phone on the floorboard without the strangers getting to him first.

"SHUT THIS BUS DOWN, OLD MAN!"

The driver had no choice. He turned and looked back at the twenty or so kids in the bus. Fear was plastered across their faces, and he knew that his fate and the fate of the children were in the hands of two very evil strangers.

Edward turned the key to the left, and the bus shut down. He looked up at one of the strangers just in time to see a large fist collide with his nose. The back of Edward's head hit the driver's-side window, knocking him unconscious as he slouched over the steering wheel.

A few children screamed and got up from their seats but stopped when Kelvin stepped into the aisle and glared at them all menacingly. "All of you shut up! If we hear anyone speak so much as a word, we'll destroy you and the person sitting next to you. Now, we're looking . . . STOP THAT WHIMPERING . . . we're looking for Ethan Franklin. Is he on this bus?"

"STOP CRYING!" Sickle shouted impatiently.

"IS HE HERE OR ISN'T HE? WHERE IS ETHAN FRANK-LIN?" Kelvin roared.

A boy sitting in the back of the bus stood up slowly.

"You — boy. Are you Ethan?"

"Yes," came his quiet response.

"Get up here."

Ethan scooted out into the aisle. Every petrified eye was staring at him as he slowly took a step forward.

"Come on — move it!"

Suddenly, there came a knock, and Kelvin and Sickle turned toward the closed bus doors. Standing and pounding her fist loudly on the door was a girl with long, dark brown hair.

"What is this?" Sickle said, kicking the doors open. "What do you want?"

Samantha stepped forward — her heart nearly in her throat. "I'm waiting for my sister. She gets off here," she said innocently.

"Get out of here," Sickle said coldly.

As quickly as she could, Samantha donned her Vest. Thankfully, Sickle wasn't fast enough. With all her might, Samantha kicked the Dark Vest in the knee and pulled her off the bus by her shirt collar. Kelvin raised his arm, ready to blast her with a ball of flame, but was hit violently by what felt like a small truck. The force of the blow shot him backwards, through one of the large windshields of the bus, onto the street, leaving him bloody and unconscious.

Samantha kicked Sickle three more times in the midsection and with one last powerful blow to the head, watched the girl's eyes roll back into unconsciousness just as Jazmin and Nathaniel rushed up.

"Samantha! Where's the other one?" Jazmin asked in a rush.

"Lying in the street." Samantha pointed.

Nathaniel stared at the unconscious body at his feet while Jazmin ambled over to the fallen Dark Vest in the street. "How'd that guy end up out here on the road?" Jazmin asked, now standing over the limp body of Kelvin.

Ethan walked down the steps slowly and stared at Samantha and Nathaniel, both of whom were wearing Vests of Light like his. "I hit him with everything I had," Ethan whispered. "Ran as fast as I could and put my shoulder into him."

"Ethan Franklin?" Nathaniel asked gently.

"Yes," Ethan answered, grimacing as he rubbed his shoulder.

"You all right?" asked Nathaniel.

"Yeah, I think so. What's going on?"

"Ethan . . . all I can say is this was not the way we wanted you to be introduced to our world. Facing Dark Vests like this . . . we're lucky no one was hurt."

Ethan looked utterly confused.

"Welcome, Ethan."

"To what?" Ethan asked as Jazmin made her way over.

All of the students in the bus crammed over to the right side, sliding the windows down and watching Ethan carefully.

"Welcome to the Brilliants."

"The what?"

Jazmin withdrew a golf-ball-sized orb from her front jeans pocket. "We'll explain everything in a moment."

"Get rid of these guys first," Nathaniel said, motioning to the unconscious Dark Vest.

"Where should I transport them?"

"Underground about six feet," Samantha said, half sarcastically, half seriously.

"I can't do that," Jazmin answered in a shocked voice.

"Why not? They would have killed you if they had a chance. Trust me, I know. I've fought them before."

"So have we, Samantha, and killing them is against everything we stand for as Brilliants. Jazmin, transport them to a distant mountain someplace. They won't be there long. Thry will come to get them," Nathaniel said quietly, staring at Sickle's unconscious body.

"You're going to let them go?" Samantha asked in disbelief. "Can't you send them to Banishment?"

"Only the Robe has that power," Nathaniel answered calmly.

"What about jail or something?"

"Jail wouldn't hold them."

"Don't you have a jail for Dark Vests — like a special jail? What's the point of fighting them if we let them go and they come back to fight against us another day? This is so stupid," Samantha said in a rage. "Maybe it's time the Maker made something that can hold Dark Vests!"

"A very good idea, Samantha," Nathaniel conceded. "He's talked about doing something like that for years. Perhaps now is the time. As for these two — they must be transported out of the immediate area. Jazmin, transport them."

In two great flashes of bright light, the bodies disappeared. The children on the bus gasped simultaneously.

"Throw it now," Nathaniel commanded.

"What about the bus driver?" Ethan asked, staring up at Edward.

"He's all right," Samantha said, analyzing him with her Vest. "He won't remember a thing after Jazmin throws it."

"Throws what?"

Jazmin brought the orb to her mouth, whispered, and then threw it to the ground. The explosion of light forced everyone to shut their eyes, and when they opened them a few seconds later, the four Brilliants were standing in the Maker's quarters.

"What the . . ." Ethan gasped, looking out the window and staring at an orbiting earth.

"I promise we'll explain everything in a minute, Ethan, but first I have to call someone." Jazmin brought her wrist to her mouth and spoke into the golden Bracelet. "Maker, we're back."

She pulled the Bracelet away from her mouth and looked at it. Almost instantly it was aglow as she stared at it, transfixed. Then she said, "Yes, of course."

A moment later there was a quick flash of light, and the Maker was standing in the room with them behind his desk. "Oh, Jazmin — wasn't quite ready for that," he chuckled, rubbing his belly. "Well, I see you've brought back Ethan . . . very good. Ethan Franklin, I'm so glad you're here. I trust everything went smoothly?"

Ethan hadn't heard a word of what the Maker had said. He was too captivated by the view.

"Things were far from smooth." Nathaniel stepped forward. "Two Dark Vests had gotten there before we did. Samantha knew right away when we saw the bus. But before we could even come up with a plan, she charged over and took one of them out. Then Ethan knocked the other one out the windshield."

The Maker looked suddenly distressed and sat down in his chair, motioning for the rest of them to sit as well.

"Ethan. Ethan!" Jazmin said, pulling on the boy's shirt.

"Huh? Yeah — yeah."

"Sit down."

"Right," Ethan said, taking a chair, although still visibly awed by the view.

"Okay," the Maker said seriously. "Samantha, I need you to understand that everything we do here is done as a team. I sent three of you because it's safer and wiser than just sending one person. Never be hasty to battle with the Dark Vests."

"But something had to be done," Samantha said defensively.

"Yes, but perhaps you could've consulted with Nathaniel and Jazmin first? I know that you've fought before, and I can see you have a strong spirit, but please be safe and wise in your decisions in the future. We cannot afford to lose you.

"Now, as for you, Mr. Franklin . . ."

"Yes?" Ethan sat up in his chair.

"We have much to talk about . . ."

PREPARATION
September 18 - 5:30 p.m.

"Spaghetti with meatballs," Jazmin said, and immediately a heaping plate of spaghetti with large meatballs appeared on the glowing plate.

Evenina looked at her plate and said, "Hamburger and fries. Everything on the burger except for onions." Just as Jazmin's had, Evenina's plate filled with her request.

"Are you going to eat, Samantha?" Jazmin asked, wrapping spaghetti around her fork before taking a bite.

Samantha looked at the glowing plate in front of her but couldn't think of anything she wanted to eat. Her mind was elsewhere, dwelling on the events that had taken place earlier.

"You okay?" Evenina asked before taking a small bite out of her hamburger.

"I think so," Samantha answered in a whisper. "Just thinking."

"About?"

"What happened with Ethan today."

Jazmin swallowed. "Hmm. Yeah."

"What did happen, anyhow?" asked Evenina in between bites.

"It was intense," Jazmin said excitedly.

"What was intense?" came Juan's voice.

Samantha looked up and saw her two best friends walking toward her.

"You know, you could come and get us when you're going to eat," George said, strapping a Belt around his waist and taking a chair.

Samantha smiled as Juan strapped on a Belt and sat down next to her. "Pepperoni pizza . . . sliced," he said, and his plate disappeared underneath the steaming sixteen-inch pie.

"Pizza. Half Canadian bacon and pineapple, half cheese — sliced," George said, watching his selection appear as well.

"What was intense?" Juan asked again, taking a slice. "Did you get Ethan?"

"Barely," said Samantha gravely. "We got there just in time to stop the Dark Vests."

George nearly choked. "What!"

"Yeah — Dark Vests."

"Did they attack you?" asked George, sitting a little straighter in his chair.

"I attacked them," Samantha answered, like it was an everyday occurrence.

Juan shot George an I-don't-believe-it look. "You attacked a Dark Vest? Come on."

"Really, she did," Jazmin assured them. "It was quite brave."

"So what happened?" George asked, intrigued.

Samantha cracked a smile. "Well, Ethan was riding the bus home, and when we got there I knew right away that two Dark Vests had forced the bus driver to shut the bus down, so I took off my Vest and walked up to the doors and knocked really loud. One of the Dark Vests opened it and asked what I wanted, and that's when I concentrated on my Vest and . . ."

"Beat the crap out of her," Jazmin finished.

Juan and George stared at each other again.

"You're serious?"

Samantha nodded.

"What about the other Dark Vest?" Evenina asked with great anticipation.

"Ethan slammed him through the windshield of the bus and knocked the guy out."

"Whoa," Juan laughed. "That reminds me of a time I did that when I was invisible."

Samantha and George grinned.

"Mountain Dew," Evenina said, as the mug next to her plate filled to the brim. "Why don't you guys ever have your Vests on?"

"Why?" Juan shrugged. "If I had mine on all the time, I'd just be invisible. No one would see me."

"I can already pretty much fly in here, so I don't need the Gift of Flight."

Evenina nodded as she took a drink of her soda.

"I have a question about something my Vest isn't telling me," Samantha said, looking at Jazmin.

"Huh?"

"That thing you threw down on the ground . . ."

"The Forgetter," replied Jazmin quickly. "Cool, aren't they? Once I throw them on the ground, they explode and anyone who has seen what happened has their memories erased."

George pointed at her. "You used those Forgetter things at the zoo."

"Right."

"But you also had another ball. . . ."

"A Retriever. When they explode, anyone who has attempted to record any information, either visual or audio, has the equipment taken away and it's destroyed."

"Who made those?"

"The Maker. I only have a few left, though," Jazmin added, taking a mug and whispering, "Pepsi."

"How can he make all that?" Juan marveled.

"This Lighthouse took him nearly ten years to make," Jazmin said soberly, "including the Colossals, the Garden, the CTF Field . . ."

"Ten years?"

"Yeah. It nearly killed him. The fatigue he had to endure as he constructed it — nobody has experienced fatigue like him. Trust me."

"So how long did it take him to make those Forgetter things?"

"I'm not sure," answered Jazmin between sips of her Pepsi.

Juan nodded in awe. "Incredible! He's the man."

Striding over to their table was a young boy that Samantha immediately recognized as Mathias Braxton.

"Hello," he said curtly. "Mind if I sit?"

Even if anyone had minded, he wouldn't have cared. He sat down and stared at Samantha as though dazed.

"Who are you?" Samantha asked, frowning and looking at the boy.

"Who am I? Ha! I am Braxton."

"You are not!" replied the boy to himself. "You'll have to excuse him, he's a bit mental. I am Mathias."

Samantha didn't know why his Vest was a strange gray color, and before she could ask him he leaned forward and looked at their plates of pizza.

"Can't stand the pizza here. HERE! Over here!" he broke into song: *Over here, oh, my dear, I'm over here. I'm over here.*

"Samantha, dear, I'm OVER HERE!"

Everyone at the table, besides Evenina and Jazmin, who were accustomed to such behavior, looked at the boy as if he were completely mental. A few people that were eating at tables nearby told Braxton to shut up.

"You shut up. . . . Song . . . We need song!"

"What's your power?" George asked.

"Power of the mind," he drew out the last word for emphasis.

"How's that?"

The boy fixed his gaze on Samantha again. Suddenly she leaned forward over her empty plate, her eyes looking distant and foggy. The boy leaned forward, and the next thing everyone at the table saw was the two of them engaged in a kiss.

"Hey," George shouted, grabbing Braxton by the shoulder.

Braxton turned and fixed his stare on George. George suddenly let go of the boy and turned to Juan who leaned back but couldn't stop George from kissing him on the cheek.

"Get off me!" Juan said, pushing a dazed George away. "WHAT ARE YOU DOING?"

Braxton felt a cold, hard slap across the side of his face as George broke out of his stupor.

"Braxton!" Jazmin spat. "Knock that off, and don't you give me that look, or I'll send you to the Sahara Desert."

The boy stood up cheerfully. *"Thank you . . . thank you . . ."* he sang as he strode away. *"Not a bad kisser. She can kiss. Samantha can lay one on ya!"*

"What is he saying?" Samantha turned red.

Juan looked furious. "You kissed me on the cheek, George!"

George's eyes flashed. "What? Shut up."

"No, man. You did. You kissed me."

"No, I didn't. I don't remember kissing you. That's sick."

"Yeah!" Juan nodded.

"I kissed Mathias?" Samantha looked at Evenina and Jazmin.

"Yeah," Evenina said, suppressing a laugh. "Actually it was Braxton, but don't feel bad. He's done that to all the girls, except for Jaz."

"How'd he do that?" George asked, wiping his lips with the back of his hand.

"That's his power," Evenina answered. "He has the Gift of Mind Manipulation. He can make you do things you wouldn't normally do, and what's even worse is that you don't remember what you did."

"Really?"

"Yeah. It's an awesome power that he misuses all the time, which is why his Vest is gray. It's in transition. But it's been like that for awhile."

"What do you mean 'it's in transition'?" George asked.

"When someone begins to do wrong with their Vest, it begins to change from a Vest of Light to a Dark Vest. Before it actually goes black, it becomes gray, like his. It's like he's half and half — half good, half bad," Evenina explained. "When he's Braxton, he's really mischievous. And when he's Mathias, he's really good, so his Vest stays gray all the time."

"When he's Mathias? Braxton?" George was lost.

"He has a split personality. He's been that way ever since his parents died."

"Died?" Samantha said, frowning.

Evenina spoke quietly. "Xylo killed his parents in front of him about a month after he got his Gift. Messed him up bad. For about a year he wouldn't even talk, so the Maker adopted him. We try not to be too hard on him, except when he pulls stuff like he did just now."

"I would've never guessed . . ." Juan whispered. "What a power, though."

"It's an awesome power. That's why the Maker doesn't let Mathias leave the Lighthouse. If he did, who knows what he'd do — plus the Dark Vests would go after him for sure. As long as we're in the Lighthouse, we're safe."

"Samantha Banks," a deep voice resonated from across the Banquet Hall. Standing in the entryway was Septimus. He was gesturing her over with one hand.

"Looks like I've got to go," she said, standing.

"Where?" George asked.

Samantha squinted and used her power of knowledge. "Time for practice," she whispered.

"Practice?"

"CTF."

"Huh?" George looked at Juan.

"Capture the Flag," Samantha said, stepping around the

table. "Sorry I didn't tell you. Forgot about it."

"What the heck is it?" Juan wanted to know.

"Umm, have Jazmin explain," Samantha said, walking off toward Septimus.

"I have a lot to go over with you guys. Didn't Lance already tell you about Capture the Flag?"

"No," said Juan and George at the same time.

"Okay, this Capture the Flag is unlike anything you've ever seen. . . ."

Samantha, meanwhile, was listening to Septimus as they walked along the corridor. "We've got only one practice to get you ready for tomorrow's tournament. However, I figured since you have the Vest of Knowledge, it shouldn't be too difficult."

They floated down to the first floor and made their way to the massive golden doors.

"Where are we going?" Samantha asked, stepping back as the right hand door opened to the touch of one of the gargantuan Colossals. As they slipped past, Samantha had to stop and stare one more time at their grandeur.

"We're going to the CTF Field where the game is played — there." Septimus pointed, and in the distance she could see two towers: one green, one red. "I'll explain as we walk."

"I think I know how to play," Samantha said, taking two steps for every one of his.

"Good. Explain."

"There are two teams, a red and a green. The two towers are open-faced and have three levels. The flag is in the middle level. Each team must try and steal the other team's flag without losing their own flag."

"Good, keep going."

"Our own Vests don't work once we step onto the Field, so we have to open one of the three Chests before the game starts. And you want me to open . . ."

". . . the Chest that is marked EYES."

"Right. That will give me the Gift of Vision."

"That's correct," Septimus said, nodding. "What else?"

"All of us also have the ability to shoot balls of light from our hands and if one of the balls hits the opposing team, it will send them back to their base at the bottom level."

"What about the enhancements?"

Samantha continued smoothly. "Those are the Speed Skates and the Rocket Anchor. Either one of them will get me across the Field really fast."

They were now facing a wall of what looked like water flowing in every direction. It completely encompassed the Field in an enormous liquid-like bubble.

"Once you step through, your power of knowledge is useless. You understand?" Septimus asked, staring down at Samantha.

"Yes."

"Let's go then."

Septimus stepped through the water wall and Samantha followed. It felt as though she walked through a large cloud of light blue dust. When she had passed completely through, she found herself standing on green grass cut low and even. The entire Field looked like a manicured golf course fairway. Walking toward her was a tall, thin boy.

"Brent Quincy, meet Samantha Banks," Septimus said as the two shook hands.

"Hi."

"Nice to meet you," Brent said politely.

Samantha had a sudden urge to use her Vest to find out more about her new teammate, but realized it had vanished.

"Follow me," Brent said, leading her toward the open-faced green tower.

"I'll be the target," Septimus said, walking toward the red tower.

"So we've only got one practice to get you ready for tomorrow's match," remarked Brent.

"Yeah."

"Having the Vest of Knowledge helps," Brent said as they made their way into the entry, "but as you know, once you're on the Field, it's useless."

As they rounded the corner, Brent moved to his right and that's when Samantha saw them. Three Chests, very similar to the one she had seen in Boulder Cave the day she received her Gift, were lined up against the wall.

"That first one there is the one Septimus will open tomorrow. That's the Gift of Flight. The second one — the transparent one — that's the Chest with the Gift of Invisibility. I'll open that one, and yours is the last one. See the markings right below the latch? EYES. That's you."

"Should I open it?" asked Samantha hesitantly.

"Go ahead."

She walked forward and stared. What was going to happen? Would she see a blast of white light like she had in Boulder Cave? Would she hear the thundering voice? She looked over her shoulder at Brent.

"It's okay. Open it," he said with a smile.

Samantha drew a breath and pushed the lid open. Just like the Chest in Boulder Cave, this one was empty inside and lined with a very clean linen cloth. She was about to ask Brent what to do next when a white mist began to filter out over the edges. She had seen this before. Samantha backed up and hadn't taken more than a few steps when a bolt of light shot out.

"To you, the Gift of Sight," a powerful voice echoed.

She looked down at her chest and saw the outline of a Vest form, before disappearing quickly. As it dissolved, the smoke receded back into the Chest, and the lid slammed shut with a loud THUD. She expected it to explode into a ball of light and disappear just like in Boulder Cave.

"The Chest stays," Brent said, noticing Samantha's stare.

"They're always here. Also, your Vest is invisible, but believe me, you have it on."

"Invisible? But can't other Brilliants see it?"

"No. It's part of the game. You can't even see your own Vest, and neither can anyone else."

"Incredible," Samantha whispered.

"You need to get accustomed to your sight, so let's go back out to the Field so you can practice."

Brent directed Samantha back to the entryway. Across the grassy Field was the glimmering red tower.

"I don't see anything unusual," Samantha shrugged.

"Concentrate on your new power just like you do with knowledge. Concentrate on sight and what you want to do with the sight. Focus on staring ahead at the far tower and zooming in on Septimus. He's probably on the very top."

Samantha closed her eyes a moment and thought just as Brent had told her. When she opened them, her gaze suddenly rushed forward, and she was now looking directly into Septimus' eyes as if he were a hand's stretch away.

"I can see him," she said in amazement. "Wow!"

"Very good," she heard Septimus say. She turned her head to the right because she could've sworn that's where his voice had come from. When she did, her eyesight returned to normal.

"Wait, how can I hear you? You're on the opposite tower," she said, incredulously.

"Once you step onto the Field, you're able to communicate with each other as if we were close. It helps, especially when things start getting crazy during the match. What ear do you hear me speaking in?"

Samantha tapped her right ear. "Right."

"Then you'll hear Brent in your left. And one more thing — the opposing team will not be able to hear us communicate, unless, of course, they're standing so close they can hear you speaking."

"Okay, but if you are talking to me at the same time as Brent, that's gonna be weird."

"You'll get used to it," Brent said, smiling and walking past her out onto the Field.

"Samantha, I'm going to fly around over the Field. I want you to try to hit me with your balls of light," Septimus said in her right ear.

"How can you fly?"

"I opened the red Chest marked FLIGHT. Now, get ready."

Samantha looked down at her hands. They looked just like they always did. "How do I use my hands to shoot out light?"

"Raise them and make a fist. Each time you do, a ball of light will shoot from them in the direction you're pointing. Okay, I'm coming right at you. Use your sight — aim — and fire at me."

Samantha looked up and zoomed easily. Septimus was gliding at her in George's favorite Superman position. She raised her right arm in front of her face, squinted her left eye, and made a fist. An explosion of white jetted out of her hands and hurled toward Septimus. He didn't even have to maneuver out of the way because Samantha's aim was so poor. She had missed by twenty feet.

"Fire again," Septimus ordered.

Samantha squinted and fired again, but Septimus dodged the white glowing ball easily.

"Anticipate where you think I might be turning, and this time send a barrage. Open and close your fist as fast as you can, but don't forget to take aim. Go!"

Septimus turned hard to the left and flew toward the edge of the water-like border. Samantha focused on her power and zoomed in. Then she raised both arms, kept her left eye open, and fired as many balls of light as her palms could manage.

Nearly twenty balls of blazing white light shot forward.

Septimus wheeled around in the air and tried to gain speed to avoid them. Even though he ducked out of the way of the first two, he couldn't escape the others and was struck in the head. There was a burst of white light, and he was gone.

"That's more like it," Septimus said slowly.

"Where are you?" Samantha asked, looking around.

"Back at the bottom level of the red tower. When you get hit with a ball, you are returned to your home tower. In this case, your home tower is green, so that's where you would be returned if you got hit with a red ball. I'm going to fly out again. I want you to go to the very top of the green tower and shoot at me from up there."

"But how do I get to the top?"

There was no response. Samantha asked again, but got nothing. She turned and looked at Brent. "Okay, how do I . . ."

"Jump," he said simply.

Samantha looked up at the immense tower and thought how ridiculous "jump" sounded. There wasn't any possible way a human could come close to getting to the top level. She stared at Brent.

"That's impossible. I can't jump up there."

"Remember that the Field is not like earth. You'll be surprised at how high you can actually jump. Now, jump! Septimus is coming, and I bet this time he fires at you."

She turned back and zoomed in on the other tower. She could see Septimus emerging from the entryway. She bent her knees and jumped. It was like nothing she had expected. She was catapulted straight up, and as she ascended, realized the whole Field was a low gravity environment, similar to the Lighthouse. She veered forward and landed, standing directly in front of a four-foot, plain-green flag attached to a silver pole fastened to a glowing brass stand.

She wheeled around and looked at Brent below.

"Jump again," she heard him say in her left ear.

She nodded, looked up, and jumped again. She soared higher, this time to the very top of the tower where two green flames lit both ends of the tower, sparkling and hovering magically.

She faced the other tower and barely avoided a glowing ball that was zeroing in on her head. Septimus was firing at her, and she wasn't ready. She rolled to her left, avoiding two more balls of light before getting to her feet. She scanned the Field and the sky. Nothing. It was like Septimus had disappeared. She walked to the edge and looked down.

From the middle tier, she saw him soar away, carrying the flag in one hand. With the other, he turned and fired at her. He was playing for real, and he had her flag. She sprinted forward, leaping off the edge and soaring into the air. She concentrated hard as she gave chase, balls of light shooting out of both hands. Three of the lighted balls missed, but the fourth hit him in the foot. In a blaze of light, he disappeared and with him, the flag.

It wasn't until then that Samantha realized she was falling to the ground, but it was an easy glide and when she touched down, it felt as though she hadn't even jumped. She turned and looked up at the middle level of the green tower. Glimmering as it had been a minute before, the green flag stood. It had been returned.

★ ★ ★

"Capture the Flag sounds awesome," George said, landing softly, followed by Juan.

"Yeah. Wish we could have been in it," replied Juan as he headed toward a floating shelf of books labeled Sports.

"Wouldn't that be cool to have two powers? I would love to have Invisibility and Flight."

"Or," George said excitedly, "Flight and Speed."

"Yeah." Juan nodded as he approached the floating shelf,

trailed by George.

"Hey, fellas," came Fox's voice from behind them. George and Juan turned around.

"Hi, Fox," Juan said.

"What's goin' on?" asked George casually.

"Oh, just getting ready to study for our test," said Fox in a slightly dejected voice.

George and Juan looked at each other in a sort of panic.

"Test?" George muttered.

"Yeah, it's Monday and it's a big one. I've gotta start studying now!"

"Umm, what test?" mumbled Juan feebly.

Fox shook his head. "You guys don't have it. You haven't had classes yet. But when you take math . . . I'm warning you. It's tough."

"It's not that tough," came a pleasant voice as Alexia strode toward them. "I didn't have any troubles passing the class."

"Alexia," said Fox seriously, "not everyone is as smart as you. For some of us, math is really hard."

"Yes, well, even if it is hard for you, Fox, I know you'll do fine. You always do."

"Yeah, forget about the fact that I study more than just about anyone here."

"You think you study as much as Tom?" Alexia asked.

Fox thought about this a moment, but there really wasn't much to think about. Tom Kitts was the smartest person Fox had ever talked with, and one of the most studious students he had ever seen. "Okay, probably not as much as Tom, but I take second."

"Even in front of me?" Alexia grinned.

Fox frowned. "So, maybe third."

"Indeed."

"So, do you guys know what your classes are yet?" asked Fox, now addressing Juan and George.

"No, I don't think we've gotten a schedule yet, but we've already had one class with Septimus," George offered.

"Hmm," grunted Fox. "Well, you'll be getting your schedule soon."

"Who teaches the classes?" Juan wondered.

"The Maker, Septimus, Nathaniel, and Lance," replied Alexia.

"But what do they teach?" asked George.

"Well, Lance teaches most of the sciences, and Septimus teaches the math along with self-defense. The Maker teaches English and communications, and Nathaniel teaches the arts," the librarian replied casually.

"Lucky you don't have an algebra test soon," Fox said indignantly. "Septimus is brutal — making us take a test on the Monday after the tournament."

"I think it's a good thing," Alexia chimed in.

"Yeah, you're not the one who has to take it, are you?"

"So, there's school?" Juan threw up his hands.

"Of course, there's school," Fox said in an everybody-knows-that kind of voice.

"But not formal school like you're thinking of," Alexia added. "You actually have class about three times a week. The rest of the time is used for other training."

"Only three times a week?" Juan said enthusiastically. "I can live with that."

"Don't get excited," Fox said in a low tone. "I have more work here at the Lighthouse than I ever did in regular school. Trust me."

Juan's smiled disappeared.

"Can I help you find a book?" Alexia changed the subject.

"Tell us about the Book of Light," George said quickly.

Alexia's lips curled, and she looked at George a long time before speaking.

"Hello, Alexia?" Fox waved his hand in front of her.

"What do you want to know?" she finally said.

"Why is it so important?"

"Because it contains everything about the Brilliants. From the moment everything began up until now and even the future."

"Can we see it?" George asked, stepping forward.

"No!" Alexia crossed her arms.

"Why not?"

"It would do you no good, George. The Book of Light can only be read by those who are Musicular, and you're not."

"Can't we at least look at it?"

"Yeah, go on. Let 'em look," Fox added supportively. "Open it up for them. They've never . . . "

"Okay, okay," Alexia said in a quick whisper. "Follow me."

"I'll see you guys," Fox said, wheeling off. "I'm going to one of the study booths."

Alexia led them down an aisle and then crossed a few others, weaving in and out of floating shelves until they were finally at the door. She lifted into the air and hovered a moment before being sucked in like a piece of dirt in a vacuum. Juan and George gasped. The door cranked open and there, glowing brightly on a white bookstand, was the Book of Light.

"Whoa, that's thick," George marveled.

"Come in," Alexia said, gesturing them forward.

George and Juan entered, fixated on the book as Alexia shut the door behind them.

"Go ahead and open it."

The boys stared at each other, then at Alexia.

"Nothin' bad is gonna happen, right?" George asked hesitantly.

"Yeah, the last time George opened something, we nearly died."

"We did not nearly die," George said defensively. "As it turns out, you owe me for your power of invisibility. Let's not forget that neither you nor Samantha wanted to open the Chest in Boulder Cave."

"Uh-huh," Juan grunted. "Still . . ."

"Nothing bad will happen. Open it," said Alexia confidently.

George stepped forward and opened the thick book to the first page. There was nothing on the old, white parchment — no words or pictures of any sort. Juan looked over George's shoulder and gave a shrug. Both looked at Alexia inquisitively.

"Just listen," she whispered, putting her finger in front of her lips.

In the distance, a beautiful sound, similar to that of a French horn, echoed softly, followed by an accompanying flute. The music grew louder and more melodic and soon filled the room with reverberating, breathtaking sound.

"To us, it sounds like beautiful music and nothing more. But to a Musicular, they're words being spoken and written on the pages, even though we're unable to see them. That's why Samantha is so important. She can understand what we're hearing."

* * *

"Speed Skates," Septimus stared down at the glowing shoes that looked exactly like figure skates. "Put them on."

Samantha took off her shoes and slipped the enormous pair of white skates over her feet. "They're too big," she uttered, but before Brent or Septimus could respond, the skates shrank until they fit her feet snugly.

"Amazing," Samantha marveled.

"Now, stand up," Septimus said.

Samantha stood and knew immediately that she was floating just a few inches above the ground.

"When you have those on," Septimus said, focusing on

Samantha's eyes, "you'll have the ability to go incredibly fast. You've skated before?"

"Uh-huh."

"Good. I want you to go toward the other tower as fast as you can and then come back here. Ready . . . go."

Samantha drew in a breath and pushed off. Just like with ice-skating, she glided over the ground with incredible speed. No one could possibly run this fast except for maybe Ethan with his Vest of Speed. Within a few moments, she was at the base of the red tower.

"The skates won't work inside the two towers," Septimus said in her right ear, "so you want to stay on the grassy part of the Field. Turn and come back to us."

She did as he asked and rocketed up the Field until she slid to a stop in front of her teammates.

"You've definitely skated before," said Brent admiringly.

"My parents made me take lessons for three years."

"It shows."

"Good," Septimus said, and he motioned for Samantha to sit down. "Take them off, and we'll practice with the Rocket Anchor next. But as you can tell, putting the skates on and taking them off takes time; the opposing team, if they're smart, will see this and try to take you out with a blast of light. If they do hit you with a ball of light, you'll lose the Skates. If you find them, put them on as fast as you possibly can. There're no laces, and all you have to do is push them off your feet. There, good, just like that."

"Okay, now the Rocket Anchor," Samantha said, putting on her tennis shoes and standing up enthusiastically.

"Time's up, Septimus. We have the Field now."

Three boys walked toward them, all of whom Samantha recognized from the Banquet Hall as Tom Kitts, Seth Taylor, and Pete Harris — handsome Pete Harris. Septimus looked at his watch and grumbled. "Didn't realize the time — went over.

We'll go to one of the training rooms and talk strategy. Let's go."

"Good luck tomorrow," Pete said kindly as Samantha followed Brent and Septimus off the Field. "How'd practice go?"

Samantha felt her face go red. "Okay, I guess."

"Hey, I'm done with practice at nine tonight. You want to meet in the Banquet Hall? Have some ice cream or somethin'?" Pete asked sweetly.

"Ah, sure," Samantha replied shyly.

"Great. See you up there at nine."

"Okay. Bye," Samantha said.

"Bye." Pete waved.

Septimus looked at Samantha with a grin as they passed through the wall of liquid and off the Field.

"What?" Samantha said, feeling a bit embarrassed.

"Nothin'," Septimus smirked. "Nothin' at all, but it kinda sounds like he asked you out on a date."

Brent, who was in front of them, kept walking but turned his head and grinned at Samantha.

"I don't think it's a date," Samantha said, uncertainly.

"Really?" Brent asked. "What do you think it is then?"

"This ought to be good," Septimus laughed.

"Well, it's a . . . a . . ." Samantha started.

"Date," Septimus finished. "I don't need a Vest of Knowledge to know that."

THE BOOK OF LIGHT
September 18 - 9:00 p.m.

"So George opens the Chest even though Samantha and I were telling him not to. At first, I was like . . . there's nothin' there, but then the light and the voice . . ."

Ethan nodded, taking a forkful of chocolate cake and sliding it into his mouth as Juan continued.

"Then George and I took off. We figured Samantha was behind us, but she ended up getting sucked down some sort of waterfall we didn't know existed and was in a different part of the cave. We got about halfway out when George realized she wasn't behind us."

George took over. "Yeah, and the bats. Bats everywhere! It was insane! We went back and tried to find her, but she was gone, so we headed to the entrance, and that's when I saw her on the opposite side, on the edge of the cliff. You should've seen her face when I went flying up there . . ."

George took a bite of his cherry pie.

"So where'd you find yours?" Juan addressed Ethan before taking a drink of milk.

"At the base of Union Creek Falls. It's a place I go every summer — along with my dog Taco. I took her down where the water pools up deep enough to swim and was just playing around. I didn't see who placed the Chest there or anything. I came out of the water, and there it was, like it'd been there the whole time."

"And then the light hit you?" George asked curiously.

"Yeah, just like what happened with you guys. It was freaky, especially when Taco took off running at light speed."

"What?"

Ethan finished the last of his cake. "Yeah, she was right next to me when the light hit, and some of it went on her. She took off like a bullet. It didn't last long, though."

"I didn't know animals could get a Vest."

"She hasn't gotten it since that day."

"Hey, there's Samantha," Juan said, standing up and waving. "Manthers, over here."

Samantha waved meekly and made her way over to a table against one of the far windows.

"Where's she going?" Juan asked, frowning.

"Oh . . ." George said in a whisper.

"Who's that?" Juan referred to the boy who was now sitting down next to Samantha. "What's she . . ."

"Looks . . . umm . . . like she's interested in someone else there, Juan." Ethan grinned.

"But . . . it's us. She's supposed to sit . . ." Juan looked at George unbelievingly.

"Yeah . . ." George said reproachfully.

"I'm gonna go over there and . . . "

"And what, Juan? What are you gonna say to her? She can sit there if she wants," said George.

Juan sat back down. "She doesn't even know that guy."

"You jealous?" asked Ethan quietly.

Juan was outraged. "Jealous? No. But . . . no, I'm not jealous. She just could . . . you know . . ."

Ethan and George waited.

"Nothing," Juan finally muttered, slumping in his chair.

Samantha took a bite of her strawberry ice cream and stared intently into Pete's handsome eyes. He was talking about how he had received his Gift, but she really wasn't paying much attention. She just stared at him, transfixed.

"And that's how I got my Vest," he finished before taking a spoonful of vanilla ice cream topped with hot fudge.

Samantha hadn't been listening very well, primarily because she already knew how he got his Gift of Color while traveling with his parents in Yellowstone National Park. Her Vest had at least given her that much on him. She was concentrating on his face — on his dark brown eyes and neatly combed hair.

"So, how does your power work?" Samantha asked, opting to have Pete tell her rather than use her Vest.

"I'm able to control color."

"How?"

"Root beer," Pete said as the mug in front of him suddenly brimmed with soda. "Well, let's see. Your shirt — I can change the color of your shirt from white to red."

Samantha smiled. "Really?"

"Yeah . . . take a look now."

Samantha looked down and, sure enough, her shirt was a brilliant red.

"I can change the color of almost anything besides other Vests. Here, watch this."

Suddenly, his light skin turned a dark purple and his eyes faded to gray.

"Ooh, don't do that," Samantha said, grimacing. "That does not look good."

Pete returned to his normal color. "That's my Gift," he said before taking a drink of soda. "I heard you got your Gift in a cave?"

Samantha nodded. "Uh-huh. Juan, George, and I were exploring Boulder Cave near our house when we found the Chest."

"That's unique that the Chest gave out three different Gifts. I don't think that's ever happened before."

Samantha nodded, not knowing what to say. Pete continued on.

"Do you like your power of knowledge?"

Samantha grabbed a mug and said, "Pepsi." She took a drink before answering. "I really like my Gift, although I don't enjoy the fatigue."

"Me neither. That's why I like it here in the Lighthouse. No fatigue."

Samantha nodded.

"Excuse me, I'm sorry to interrupt you two," a voice said. "I haven't gotten a chance to meet you yet, Sa-mantha. I'm the librarian. My name is Alexia Pearson."

Alexia stuck out her hand, and Samantha shook it politely.

"Hi, Alexia," Pete said.

"Hello, Pete," Alexia said crisply. "Samantha, I was wondering if maybe later you might stop by the Library. I've been meaning to talk with you. . . . "

Alexia looked at Pete, then back at Samantha.

Samantha nodded her head. "Sure."

"Great . . . just come on up when you finish. You won't have trouble finding me."

"Do you want to join us?" Pete offered politely.

"No, I'm not much of a dessert eater. I need to get back to the Library. Thanks anyway," Alexia said with a smile before walking away.

"She takes the Library way too seriously," Pete said, shaking his head in disapproval. "She's up there every waking minute."

* * *

Melt was staring at a thirty-five-inch view screen that was embedded in the wall at eye level with him. He was studying red dots that flashed across the screen, each dot representing a Dark Vest. He was about to zoom in on two dots when he heard a knock on the stone door behind him.

He turned. "Come."

The door shifted to the left, and in walked two Dark Vests.

"I was beginning to wonder about the two of you," he said skeptically. "What information have you found?"

"Not a thing," answered Fury. "There's nothing about this boy. No records, previous addresses — and trying to find a close relative's a joke. Why are we chasin' this kid?"

"Because," Melt grunted, "Xylo wishes it, and his power would be useful. He would be easy to bring over to our side."

"Fury's right, Melt. There's nothing," sixteen-year-old Water added. "The information we found about him was stuff you already knew. The Brilliants have him hidden well."

Melt slammed his fist on the table angrily. "Have you nothing to give me? I have to meet with Xylo soon, and he wants information."

Water and Fury looked at each other, grinning wickedly.

"What is it?" Melt said, frowning. "What did you find out?"

"Well, we gave up on Mathias after awhile and decided to find out about Ethan Franklin after he escaped Kelvin and Sickle."

"And . . ."

"And," Fury said slowly, "we found something very interesting when we inspected his home."

"What?" Melt was in no mood to play games.

"The Rod," Fury whispered.

Melt stared wide-eyed as Water brought the blue, ruler-sized rod out from beneath his thick jacket.

"I don't believe it," Melt said in wonder. "So it does exist."

"Thought you'd be pleased." Fury's smile widened.

"Perfect. This is perfect," Melt said, walking over and taking the Rod from Water. "You have done well, both of you."

"Xylo will be pleased?"

"You will both be rewarded for this," expressed Melt, holding the Rod up to one of the blue Eternal Flames that lit the circular, stone room. "Everything is working out better than we could've ever anticipated. With this, along with Malavax capturing two more Laxinti . . ."

"What?" Water gasped. "She found two more? That means

"there's only one left."

"One more," Melt whispered.

"One more what?" came Malavax's voice as she rounded the door and entered the room.

Water and Fury turned around and stared admiringly.

"What are you two looking at?"

"You found two more Laxinti?" Water asked, obviously in awe.

"Yes, where have you been?"

"Finding this," Melt said, holding up the Rod in front of him.

"Is that . . . ?"

"It is." Melt grinned. "The Rod of Recall."

"I didn't think it really existed."

"This is it, all right. Look at the glow. The Brilliants don't stand a chance once you've found the last Laxintoth. I take it your arm is fine?"

"Fingust healed it the moment he got there. It's normal."

"What happened?" asked Fury.

"One of the Laxinti hit me with its light, and my arm shriveled up, but I managed to call Fingust before I passed out."

Melt laughed sinisterly. "Now all we need to do is get into the Lighthouse."

★ ★ ★

Dessert (really Samantha's date) had been perfect. She had talked with Pete comfortably as they ate ice cream and shared stories about their lives. The only downer had been Juan's nasty looks from across the hall, which Samantha caught out of the corner of her eye from time to time. She had met a new friend — no, more than a friend. At least, that's what she hoped. But it had only been the first date, if you could even call it that.

Samantha landed softly and stared around at the amazing

sight. It was her first time in the Library, and she was in awe. Floating shelves of glowing books surrounded her. This was unlike any Library she'd ever been in before. She made her way through the maze of floating shelves until she finally found Alexia, shelving texts in the Geography section.

"Hi, Alexia."

"Oh, you made it. Thanks for coming," Alexia said, putting the last book onto the shelf. "I wasn't sure if you were coming. It's getting a little late."

"Pete and I talked a long time," Samantha said, grinning. "Is there a curfew on weekend nights? I know last night we had a message on the screen . . ."

"No, not on Friday and Saturday nights, at least not like weekdays. You can be up until one before you have to be in bed. But that's only for Brilliants age twelve and up. If you're under twelve, you have to be in bed by ten-thirty. You're okay," Alexia replied.

"That's good," Samantha said with relief.

"You could've asked your Vest about that, couldn't you?"

"Yeah," Samantha replied, "I just didn't focus."

"So, what do you think of the Library?"

"It's amazing," Samantha said, motioning to the surrounding shelves.

"I was wondering — hoping really — that you'd do something for me," Alexia said.

"Sure. What do you need?"

Alexia paused momentarily as if she was debating whether to ask or not. "What do you know about the Book of Light?"

"Jazmin told me a little about it in my room. My Vest tells me that it is the most important book in the Library. It contains the complete history of how the Brilliants and Dark Vests came to be. It also contains the secrets of the Weavers and the Laxinti."

"Who wrote the book?" asked Alexia.

Samantha waited on her Vest. "No one. It writes itself." She didn't realize how strange that sounded until she had said it. "It's a living book. It writes as time passes, and it also gives clues to the future."

"And . . ." Alexia prodded.

"I'm the only one who's Musicular. I'm the only one who can understand it, and you want me to read it, don't you? You want me to read the end, the last few pages."

Alexia stepped closer. "We've been losing Brilliants, and we need something — anything to give us an advantage against the Dark Vests. You can give us the advantage we need."

Samantha nodded with her eyes closed. "Where's the Book now?"

"Come, I'll take you."

The two girls meandered their way through the labyrinth of shelves and aisles until finally reaching the door to the room housing the special Book.

"This will take just a sec. I'm the only one who can pass, and the only way you can open the door is from the inside."

"I can pass, too," Samantha said simply.

Alexia looked baffled.

"I am Musicular; therefore, I can pass through the door."

"I don't think . . ." Alexia started but Samantha didn't let her finish. She stepped toward the door and was sucked in. Alexia followed.

"I didn't know you could do that," Alexia marveled.

"So, this is it?" Samantha asked, staring at the glowing Book.

Alexia nodded.

"I don't know why, but I'm nervous," Samantha admitted, clenching her fists.

"So am I," whispered Alexia.

Samantha stepped forward and opened the Book to the back, to the last few pages. She stared down at the thick parchment and saw wild flashes of white light burst out all over the page. Then, softly in the distance, she heard it — music. The sound was of a lone cello, playing deeply and smoothly.

The music became louder and she leaned over the pages because that's what it was telling her to do. The music was turning into language: *See the Gift given to you and use it wisely.*

The white page blurred with colors and for a moment, Samantha was wondering if she was having trouble seeing. But the picture cleared, and when it did, she saw herself with her Vest in a dark place. Next to her stood Juan and George.

She was in Boulder Cave, she thought. But Boulder Cave wasn't that big. Then she watched the page as silhouettes began to emerge from the background. Black, dark shadows were closing in on her and her two friends. Her hands started to shake and her mouth filled with saliva. She realized that the silhouettes were men in Dark Vests. They had her, George, and Juan pinned down.

One of them was stepping closer, although Samantha couldn't make out his face. He was pointing and seemed to be saying something; but as much as Samantha concentrated on the page, she couldn't hear his words, only the sound of the soft cello playing in the background.

A black light suddenly struck her in the stomach and she watched herself fall on her knees, as did Juan and George. She looked like she was in pain and cried out as the Dark Vests closed in around her.

Even though she was only watching, the sight of it was making her sick. A very evil feeling crept into her veins, and she had the urge to shut the Book, but before she could, the cello's song turned into words again:

Fear not. For behold . . .

And she watched herself on the page as a magnificent burst of yellow light surrounded her and emerging from the back of her long Vest was the upper body of a man — an archer —

made completely of light.

The Dark Vests began to back away as the archer pulled arrows from his quiver and fired them at the black silhouettes. The page quickly became a mixture of black and yellow until it exploded into light so bright that Samantha had to shut her eyes. The cello pounded the notes furiously, and when she opened her eyes again, she stared in horror. Running down the page were streaks of what looked like blood.

"What is it? What's wrong?" Alexia asked, staring at Samantha desperately.

"Shut it," Samantha shrieked. "Shut it!"

Alexia stepped forward and slammed the Book closed.

Samantha was almost in tears. There was something very evil about what she had just seen, the Dark Vests and the sight of the blood running down the page.

"What is it? What did you see?"

"I need to get out of here," Samantha cried, wheeling around and opening the door.

"Samantha . . . wait," Alexia called, grabbing her by the arm. "What did you see?"

Samantha tried to gather herself. "I saw — I saw myself, George, and Juan and we were in — in a huge cave and we were surrounded by Dark Vests. They shot beams of black light at us. Then out of the back of my own Vest came a man with a bow and arrows. He was made of light, and he started firing arrows everywhere. Then there was all this black and yellow light and — and then blood began to run down the page."

Alexia stood transfixed. "Blood?"

"Blood."

"Do you know . . ."

"I don't know what any of it means. My Vest isn't telling me anything. But I do know this, Alexia. It was the future because that's never happened. The Dark Vests we fought were in a barn, and there were only three of them. I've never seen a man made of light carrying a bow come from my back. What I saw was the future."

"Perhaps, but not everything you see in the Book of Light comes to pass," Alexia said, trying to be reassuring.

"Are you sure? How do you know? You're not Musicular."

CAPTURE THE FLAG
September 18 - 11:00 p.m.

"You okay, Manthers?" Juan asked as he and George landed softly on the ground next to the flowing Fountain of Light. "Evenina told us you wanted to meet at the Fountain."

"Yeah, what's up? We were about to go to bed," George asked, concerned.

"You wanna walk a bit?" she said quietly.

Juan and George looked at each other. "Okay, what's going on?" asked Juan. "This isn't about that Pete guy, is it?"

"What?" Samantha cracked a smile. "No, why? Jealous?"

"Shut up," Juan retorted quickly.

Samantha led the two boys to the massive doors, and just as she stopped, the left door opened with the help of one the Colossals. They walked out and into the open carpet of light. In the distance, the earth shone brightly along with millions of distant stars.

"Where are we going?" George wondered aloud.

"No place, really. I just wanted to get out for awhile."

Juan grabbed Samantha by the arm and stopped her. "Something's bothering you. What is it?"

Samantha swallowed hard. "I went up to the Library and met with Alexia. We went into the room with the Book of Light, and I opened it."

"Really?"

Samantha nodded. "I turned to the very back of the Book, and I saw the future, at least I think it was the future."

"And?" George was motioning with his hand for her to continue.

"And I saw the three of us trapped by Dark Vests. They were

all around us and we were all hit with black light, and then out of my Vest came the upper body of a man, like an archer. He was made of light, and he began shooting arrows at the Dark Vests. There was a bunch of light and dark and then an explosion — and then — then blood ran down the page."

"What?" George whispered.

"That's when I told Alexia to shut the Book."

"Blood? What's that mean?" asked George apprehensively.

"I don't know. I've been asking my Vest that ever since I left the Library, and I get nothing."

"So that means what? That we're going to be surrounded by the Dark Vests?" Juan asked.

"I don't know, but I thought I should tell you. I don't want you guys to get hurt because of me." She paused. "Don't you want our lives back? Before the Chest and everything? Because of us, three boys died in the barn that day. I think about that all the time and that I was responsible for their deaths."

"Now wait a minute." George stepped up. "You weren't responsible for their deaths. You didn't kill them."

"No, but they were there to meet us, and if we hadn't opened that Chest, they'd still be alive."

"You mean, if I hadn't opened the Chest," George corrected her. "If you want to get technical, I was the only one that opened it. If anything, Samantha, I'm really the one responsible for their deaths. You two warned me, but I didn't listen."

"Both of you stop it!" Juan broke in. "It's nobody's fault those boys died. If we wanted to blame someone, we could blame lots of people . . . the Maker or the Will for sending them there . . . but that's not what we're supposed to be doing. Everything happens for a reason, and right now we don't know what that reason is. Maybe someday we will. I'm not scared about whatever it is you saw, Manthers. As far as I'm concerned, you write your own future, and mine isn't written yet. I don't regret getting my Vest, even though I regret that those three guys died. We're supposed to be here — you especially."

"Me?"

"Don't pretend like you can't feel it," Juan said seriously. "Everyone's talking about you, about how you're Musicular, and how you will be able to help defeat the Dark Vests. I mean, you're even playing in the CTF tournament tomorrow. And did you see the way Septimus looked at you when you kicked him during training? You're it, Samantha. Don't ever regret that you received your Gift of Knowledge. I don't know about George and me, but you were supposed to get that Gift. You were *meant* to get that Gift."

George was nodding. "He's right. Your Vest is so important, Samantha, you can't get scared now. You can't worry that something bad is going to happen."

There was a long pause as the three looked at each other. Juan finally broke in lightly. "Now, tell us about Pete. What's up with that?"

Samantha and George laughed hard, and it was a much needed laugh, as the coming days would prove.

* * *

When Samantha sat down with George, Juan, and Ethan at the table the next morning, she didn't feel like eating much. As though yesterday's experience in the Library wasn't enough to worry about, the fact that the Capture the Flag tournament started in thirty minutes, didn't help matters.

Her night's sleep had been a wave of images, everything from blood running down the Book of Light to a strange, tingly sensation in her body as she heard what she thought sounded like xylophone chords chiming in the background, similar to those she had heard in the Music Room.

"You look like crap," George said in a brotherly tone.

"Thanks," Samantha replied, not bothering to move the long bangs that flopped in front of her eyes.

The Banquet Hall was packed with Brilliants, mostly sitting at tables in teams.

"You nervous?" Juan asked, stuffing a forkful of pancake in his mouth.

"A little. Orange juice — full."

"You're not gonna eat?"

"No, not really hungry," she replied, taking the mug filled with very cold, fresh orange juice.

"Do you know who you play first?" George asked before eating a spoonful of Fruit Loops.

Samantha nodded and finished her gulp. "We play team four: Valerio, Marcus, and Mark."

"Who are those guys? Have we met them?" Ethan asked.

"Yeah, I think so," replied George.

"How many games do you have to win to get to the championship?" Juan wondered, looking at Samantha.

"Well, there are eight teams, and we're in the first bracket. If we can win two matches, we'll play for the championship."

"I'm still a little confused about this whole thing," Ethan admitted. "You play against each other, and the winning team gets another power, right? A second Gift?"

"Right."

"And this tournament happens every five years?"

"Right," Samantha answered again.

"When was the first ever tournament?" Ethan wondered as he took a bite of huckleberry pie, something he rather enjoyed at breakfast.

"I don't know. But I do know if we win and get a second power, it's going to cause more fatigue. I'm not really sure I want that," Samantha said honestly, taking another drink of juice.

"Well, you don't have much choice now, unless Walden gets

better."

"He's still really sick. He's got the chicken pox," Samantha said, finishing the last of the juice.

"Chicken pox?"

"Yeah." Samantha shrugged. "Apple juice — full."

"Thirsty?" Juan said sarcastically.

"Yep," Samantha said, taking a drink.

"The tournament starts at ten, right?" Ethan asked, putting his fork down on the plate. "Where's the game actually going to be played?"

Samantha answered, "In the CTF Field. At ten, everyone in the Lighthouse will be transported there to watch."

"How do you know that? Because of your Vest of Light, huh?" Ethan motioned.

"No. It was on my message screen in my room. Didn't you see it this morning?"

"Didn't look," Ethan admitted. "Forgot about that."

"You better eat something. You only have a few minutes left now," George said, staring down at his watch.

"I'm okay. I'll just wait here until I'm transported."

"We'll wait with you," Juan said, finishing the last of his breakfast.

They didn't have to wait long before a flash of light blinded everyone. When they opened their eyes, they were hovering over the green, grassy playing Field. They were high, way up high, sitting in circular pods that floated smoothly in the air. Each pod had a dozen cushiony chairs that glowed with an intense gold color.

"Nice chairs," Juan said admiringly, sitting down and leaning back comfortably.

"This is awesome up here. Look, there's Jazmin over there with Alexia and Evenina," Samantha said, waving.

"So, what if we fall out of these things?" George said, staring at the ground far below.

"Don't," answered Juan. "Long way down, man."

"Yeah."

"We watch the matches from up here?" Ethan asked.

"Right," Samantha answered, staring at the other floating pods.

"But aren't you supposed to be on the Field or something?"

Samantha shook her head. "We'll be transported to the base of our tower when the match begins. Septimus told me how it works."

"Cool," Ethan said.

"Welcome, everyone," a familiar voice boomed in the distance. High above the center of the Field emerged another circular pod, and standing on it was the Maker, his voice somehow amplified.

"This marks another five-year cycle and with it, a Capture the Flag tournament. I wish all of you good luck. Players, you know the rules. Please stick to them. I haven't yet had to remove anyone from a game for misconduct, so let's not start today.

"Team one: Xavier, Magnus, and Dean . . . red tower."

And just as soon as the Maker said "red tower," the three boys were blasted away by a flash of light.

"Whoa. So they're at the red tower over there?" Ethan pointed as Juan and George looked on.

"Yeah," answered Samantha.

"And team two: Kelsey, Naomi, Rachel . . . green tower."

The three girls disappeared from their pod.

"Each team has the next two minutes to decide on positions. At the end of the two minutes, I will say 'Begin' and you are free to start. Again, good luck, all of you," the Maker said joyfully, stretching out his arms.

"You're gonna have to help me along as I watch this," Ethan said, stretching his neck to see the ground below. "I'm not sure

I fully understand."

"Neither do we," Juan admitted. "We've learned just by talking with other people."

"Did you ever think anything like this was possible?" Ethan asked.

"I thought the Lighthouse was incredible! This is freakin' awesome! How did the Maker make all of this?" George stared around in awe.

"A lot of fatigue," Samantha said in a whisper. "I wouldn't want his power."

"Oh, come on," Ethan argued good-naturedly. "You wouldn't want the ability to make anything? What if you could trade powers with him, would you?"

"I wouldn't trade my power of knowledge for anything."

"Ah," Ethan grunted.

"Would you?" she asked.

"Heck yes. I like speed and everything, but the power to make stuff . . ."

"Yeah," George nodded. "I'd trade."

"Me, too," Juan added.

"Well, I wouldn't," Samantha said strongly. "I like my power too much."

George was about to tell Samantha she was nuts when Juan blurted out: "Here they come."

"Look at them," said George in wonder. "They're glowing red."

"That wasn't like it was in practice," Samantha said, sitting up straighter to get a better look.

"And here comes the other team. They're glowing green." Juan pointed as two green players charged out onto the grassy Field.

What came next was a blitz of red and green luminescent balls exploding in every direction as the players began to attack each other.

"The balls of light weren't colored in practice, either!" observed Samantha.

"Well, they are now," Ethan said, clapping. "Go green!"

"Green? You want green?" Samantha looked at him strangely. She hadn't thought about actually rooting for a team.

"Yeah, Rachel's cute." Ethan let out a smile.

"Uh-huh," agreed Juan, not taking his eyes off the Field.

A green ball of light hit Xavier in midair, sending him back to the base of his tower. Almost at the exact same time, Naomi, who was using her Gift of Sight to zoom in, didn't notice Dean approach from her left and was hit by a ball of red and disappeared back to her green tower.

"This is awesome," George shouted. He turned to Samantha. "I wish I could play."

"I would let you play for me if it were my decision."

"Whoa, check it out. Someone's got the red flag." Ethan pointed.

"Where is it?"

"There, coming out of the bottom of the red tower. It's the person with the Gift of Invisibility, 'cause I don't see a body . . . just the flag. That looks really weird," Ethan laughed.

"Look at that!" Juan whispered in amazement.

"Go! Go! Almost there, almost there," hollered George, rising up in his seat as if this was going to help the person carrying the flag to score.

And score the green team did.

"Game," sounded the Maker's voice. "Great game. Winning team of Kelsey, Naomi, and Rachel advance to play the winner of match two between Samantha, Brent, and Septimus and Valerio, Marcus, and Mark."

Before Samantha had a chance to even say good-bye or to hear George, Juan, and Ethan wish her good luck, she was standing at the base of the red tower.

"Each team has two minutes for preparation . . ." she heard

the Maker boom in the distance.

To her left, Septimus stepped forward toward the Chests of Light, as did Brent to her right.

"Open your Chests," Septimus told them.

Samantha stared at the Chest labeled EYES and pulled the lid open. Almost immediately a thick, red smoke emerged and a beam of hot red light shot into her chest: "To you, the Gift of Sight."

She looked down and was amazed to see her clothes completely covered in shimmering red sparkles. She turned and looked at Septimus who was also glittering red from head to toe.

"Brent, you here?" Septimus asked.

"Right here," he called, close by.

"Okay, remember your positions. Good luck."

There was only a short wait before the Maker said, "Begin."

"Let's do this," Septimus shouted, bolting away with Samantha close behind.

As she reached the entryway and her foot touched the first blades of grass, she stopped and stared above her. The Field, the floating pods, the glowing players — it was all so incredible. It was truly unbelievable. There was an exhilarating feeling in the air, and it had bitten her. She was thrilled to be playing this game.

"Quit gawkin'!" she heard Brent shout as he ran by her invisibly.

Samantha leapt into the air, soaring higher until she was in the middle of the tower where her team's red flag stood motionless. She wheeled around to face the opposing team but barely had time to duck out of the way as a ball of green sailed toward her face.

Flying directly at her was a boy with short black hair who reminded her of Juan. He was coming fast, and leading him were balls of green light, all heading toward her. She tried to avoid them, but there were too many and one caught her in the knees. All she could see was a brilliant flash of green. Within seconds, she found herself at the base of the red tower. This meant there wasn't anyone guarding her team's flag.

She sprinted through the entryway and used her Gift of Sight to focus in on the boy who had hit her with a ball of green light. He was high above, nearly halfway across the Field; in his hands was the red flagpole, the red flag flapping wildly. He was flying fast. To try and shoot him would be useless. He was too far away. Samantha turned her attention to the green tower's entryway, because running forward and carrying the green flag invisibly was Brent and right behind him, Septimus.

Septimus ascended into the air, and there was a massive exchange of green and red balls as he attacked the red flag carrier. Samantha stared, hoping that Septimus had gotten him and returned the red flag back to the red tower. Behind her, she caught a glimpse of red light and knew Septimus had been hit with a green ball and sent back.

"What are you doing?" he yelled. "Defend Brent. He's coming!"

"But they got our flag!"

"No! I got him just as he got me. The red flag's been returned, but they haven't hit Brent yet!" Septimus said while running onto the Field.

Samantha trailed him and watched as he blasted balls of red light toward the oncoming players.

"Fire, Samantha!" he said in a rage.

Samantha had forgotten that she too had the ability to fire, and Brent was getting closer as balls of red and green burst everywhere around them. She focused on the flying boy who was bearing down on Brent with a barrage of green balls. She took a step and jumped into the air, using her Gift of Sight to help her. She focused and fired two glowing red balls from her hands.

The first one missed high, but the second one found its target and sent the boy away in an eruption of red light.

Septimus' found his target, too, because the other green player was transported back to the green tower at almost the same time. This cleared the way for Brent as he leapt into the air, soaring toward the middle level of the red tower and scored.

"Game," came the Maker's voice. "Very good game. Winning team of Samantha, Brent, and Septimus advances to play Kelsey, Naomi, and Rachel. Our next game is between teams five and six. Mathias, Garret, and Charlie versus Vic, Fox, and Jacob."

The next moment, Samantha found herself back in the pod with Juan, George, and Ethan, who were all congratulating her.

"That was awesome!"

"You were great!" Juan shouted, giving her a hug.

It took a few moments for Samantha to realize what had happened. She looked down at her shirt and the red sparkles had vanished.

"That was such a good shot," Ethan said enthusiastically. "I wasn't sure if you were gonna get him."

"Yeah, nice shot, Manthers," George said with a smile.

"Did you see Septimus' shot when that one guy had your flag? That was an incredible shot! They were about to score. I thought you'd lost big time," Juan said as the boys' attention was drawn back onto the Field for the start of the next match.

But Samantha's attention wasn't on the Field. It was on herself, and she felt terrible. Even though her team had won, she nearly cost them the game. If it hadn't been for Septimus' shot, they would be out of the tournament, and she didn't want to be the one responsible for that.

Why had she gotten so nervous? She had played in games before, albeit not as intense. Competition was nothing new to her. She usually thrived on it but not during that match. She had to play better. She needed to remember what Septimus said and about the strategies to use, but there'd hardly been any time to practice those strategies.

"Hey, Samantha! Did you see that?" shouted George, turning back and looking at her as the crowd cheered. "Mathias just got transported back to his tower. A green ball hit him right in the face. Oh, I can't wait to see your next match."

Her next match came sooner than she anticipated. Team Five defeated Team Six in a great match as both teams stole each other's flag more than once. In the end, it had been (surprisingly) Mathias Braxton with the Gift of Flight who secured the game for his red team.

The match between Team Seven and Team Eight had been less exciting. Samantha watched as Pete Harris with the Gift of Invisibility easily stole the red team's flag and scored. Part of her was happy for Pete and his partners but another part was sad that Jazmin, Evenina, and Alexia didn't get to move on. Samantha had also observed that not once in all the matches had she seen anyone use the Speed Skates or the Rocket Anchor.

"The Rocket Anchor and Speed Skates randomly appear and disappear throughout the game in different spots. If you're lucky, you find one of them," she remembered Septimus telling her.

She also remembered that the matches would continue without any breaks or delays, which meant that her growling stomach would have to wait until after the matches ended. With four teams remaining, that was going to be awhile.

"Samantha, your team's up," Ethan said eagerly.

"Good luck," George said.

"Yeah, pay more attention this time!" Juan smiled and then frowned. "I mean it."

Once again the Maker's voice boomed: "Team Two — Kelsey, Naomi, Rachel . . . green. Team Three — Samantha, Brent, Septimus . . . red."

In a burst of light, she found herself in front of the familiar Chest labeled EYES and just like last time, was blasted with red light until her whole body was aglow.

"This time," Septimus pointed fiercely, "you do . . ."

"I know," Samantha interrupted. "I'm ready this time."

"Good. Okay then."

"Begin."

Brent, Samantha, and Septimus sprinted together through the entryway onto the Field. Samantha didn't waste time. She bolted to the middle level and then leapt higher until she was standing on the very top tier.

"Watch behind you, Septimus," she said aloud, knowing that Septimus could hear her perfectly. "Go to your left. Left hard."

She watched him soar to his left and avoid three balls of green that Naomi had fired. It was time for her to go on the offensive. Samantha stuck her arms out in front of her and focused on Rachel who was using her Gift of Flight to propel her way to the red flag. Samantha fired a volley of red bursts from above and caught Rachel off guard. The first one missed, but the second ball found its target and sent her away in a red flash.

Samantha turned her attention to the opposite tower and used her Gift of Sight to zoom in. Septimus was making a mad dash for the green flag as the whole tower was lit up with green and red explosions. Emerging from it all was her older teammate, flying as high as possible and, clutched in his right hand, was the green flag.

"Go, go!" Samantha shouted.

"Defend me! Defend me!" Septimus shouted back in her right ear.

"Okay," she called back hurriedly.

"Got your six," she heard Brent say in her left ear.

Samantha wasn't sure what Brent meant until she saw balls of red light shoot from the ground and into the sky toward

Septimus' pursuers. "Got your six" meant Brent had Septimus' back covered, and his blasts halted whatever chance the green team had of winning.

"Game to Samantha, Brent, and Septimus," shouted the Maker as Septimus, still holding the green flag, touched down next to the red flag. "The other semifinal game between Mathias, Garret, and Charlie and Pete, Tom, and Seth will begin now."

Just as before, Samantha found herself transported from the playing Field to the pod where Juan, George, and Ethan again swarmed her.

"One more . . . one more . . ." George kept repeating enthusiastically.

Samantha hadn't time to contemplate the fact that her team was in the finals. She would play the winner of the current match, which meant there was a fifty-fifty chance she would face Pete. But she would have to wait nearly fifteen minutes to find out as both teams toughed it out. At one point, it looked as though Mathias' team would win, but just as Garret was about to score, he was hit with a green ball and sent back to his red tower.

In the end, it was Seth who won the game by using his Gift of Invisibility to grab the flag and zigzag his way across the Field as his two teammates shot balls of light in every direction, trying to stop his pursuers.

"What a game," George gasped. "This is it, Manthers. Whoever wins this next game, wins the tournament. Oh man, I'm nervous."

"What great matches everyone!" the Maker's voice rumbled. "Now, we come to our last match. The final game between Team Three, who will play as red, and Team Seven, playing as green. Good luck to both teams."

The next second Samantha was staring for a third time at a Chest with glowing red letters that spelled out, EYES. She drew in a breath, opened the Chest, and waited as the voice shouted:

"To you, the Gift of Sight," and she was again covered in sparkling red.

"Final game. This is it," Septimus said seriously. "You ready?"

"Ready," Samantha answered stoutly.

"I'm ready. Let's go," Brent said from somewhere, having gone completely invisible.

In the distance, Samantha heard the familiar "Begin" and the three teammates raced through the entryway. She would perch on the middle level this time and wait for the oncoming green players. She didn't need to wait long because she had barely arrived at her position when a flurry of green balls pounded toward her.

She was ready. She took two steps forward and jumped off, heading straight for Pete who was using his Gift of Flight to launch balls from the air. The move took him by surprise, and she didn't miss with her aim. The first ball of red caught him in the head and sent him back to the opposite tower.

She landed in the grassy Field and surveyed the situation. The green tower looked like a frenzy of Christmas lights. Brent and Septimus were on the attack, but were unsuccessful and were returned to the red tower, having been hit with a bombardment of green light.

"Get back up there," Septimus shouted, flying past Samantha.

She was about to leap back up to the middle level when a glistening, golden light caught her eye to the left. She turned and knew right away she was looking at the Rocket Anchor. She didn't pause, she didn't second-guess herself — she went for it. Running as hard as she could, she scooped it up and dove to her right, barely avoiding a blast of green light that sailed over her head.

She bounced up holding the Rocket Anchor in her right hand, and at the same time firing a burst of red balls at Tom

Kitts as he approached. She had to dive to her right again to avoid his blast, but this time when she bounced up, he was gone. Her light had hit him, sending him back to the green tower.

The Rocket Anchor was just as Septimus had described it when they had gone to one of the training rooms to discuss strategy. It was light and had the feel of a toy water pistol with a shaft and a cushiony trigger. The Anchor itself looked like a boat anchor, only miniaturized. It sat on a slanted piece of metal that glowed with an intense white and was propped up in the very back, slightly above Samantha's wrist.

She tried desperately to remember anything else about it, but nothing came to mind, mainly because more green balls of light were surging through the air in all different directions. It didn't help that she couldn't use her Vest of Knowledge.

Then she did something that both enraged and enthralled Septimus. Instead of guarding her team's flag, she concentrated and focused on the green tower. She closed her left eye, took aim, and pulled the trigger.

She never expected things to happen as fast as they did. First, the Anchor shot off so quickly it was a blur of luminescence speeding away and leaving a dotted trail of light linking it to the stock that Samantha held tightly. The dotted light then moved from the stock to her hips, forming a belt around her waist — all of this happening within a few seconds.

She stared hard at the trail of light and saw it lodge in the tower wall right next to the green flag in the middle level. The next moment she was racing through the air at breakneck speed, screaming at the top of her lungs. Before she knew it, she was at the green tower, standing within arm's length of the opponent's flag.

There was a strange metallic clicking sound as she looked down at her wrist, watching the Rocket Anchor fit itself back onto the metal shaft.

Pete had followed Samantha as best he could and sent a blast of green light at her. She grabbed the green flag and jumped off as glowing green balls sailed over her head, missing her by inches. As she fell gradually to the ground, she zoomed into the red tower, raised the Rocket Anchor, took aim, and fired.

Again, a dotted light appeared and formed a belt around her waist. Before she hit the ground, she was being pulled forward. The Anchor had stuck and was pulling her so fast, she had to squint to see.

What happened next was complete luck. Had Samantha aimed differently, had Seth been running in a different part of the Field, none of it would've occurred, none of it could've occurred, but it did.

As Samantha rocketed toward her tower ten feet off the ground, Seth cut across her line of ascent and, though invisible, was carrying her team's red flag. Gripping the green flag in her left hand, she held out her right arm and just as she started to ascend, wrapped her forearm around the top of the red flag, yanking it out of the grasp of the unsuspecting Seth. For a brief moment, she held both flags clumsily but then watched as the red flag exploded into light, having been transported back to the middle level of the red tower.

The scene was incredible to watch. Even more incredible for Samantha was the fact that she had just returned her own team's flag and, at the same time, was about to score and win the tournament.

She was closing in. If she could just get to the red flag before being hit with a green ball, she would win. With about fifty feet to go, she saw a green ball of light pass below her feet.

Forty feet. Thirty feet.

With only twenty feet to go, three more balls of green whizzed past her right ear, but didn't touch her. To the amazement of the crowd of on-looking Brilliants, and to the surprise of her own teammates, Samantha Banks scored.

Her team had won!

THE GARDEN OF LIGHT
September 19 - 1:00 p.m.

The Banquet Hall had been rearranged. Instead of round tables scattered everywhere, they were all neatly arranged to face toward a twenty-foot long, rectangular table which had been *made*.

"Please, please — everyone . . . The Maker stood up, raising his hands in the air. A hush fell over the Banquet Hall. "There'll be plenty of time to celebrate. I apologize for having Jazmin whisk you all away from the CTF arena like that, but I thought we might all have a bite to eat together for once, and along with it, have the winners open the Chest.

"Come up here, you three," the Maker said, pointing to Samantha, Septimus, and Brent, who stood at the center of the hall. "Everyone else, find a seat, but don't get your food until after the opening."

The winners walked forward amid handshakes and pats on the back, finally getting to the front by the rectangular table. In a bright flash of light, a Chest materialized on the table in front of the Maker. It looked like all the other Chests, old and beat up.

"This year's tournament was excellent. It's the best one I've seen in years. That move you made at the end, Samantha — that deserves a round of applause."

The Banquet Hall erupted in cheers. Even Septimus and Brent clapped vigorously. Samantha didn't figure the other Brilliants would be so kind as to applaud because, after all, they were her competition. Then she realized (without the help of her Vest) that the people in this room cared for her — they sincerely cared for her.

"Congratulations to you three and to all of you who participated. Excellent, most excellent." The Maker placed a hand on the Chest. "A second Gift is rare and comes with more fatigue. I will certainly understand if none of you want to have this. With that thought in mind, I must ask each of you . . ."

If Samantha was ever unsure she wanted a second Gift, she wasn't now. She wanted that power just as much as Septimus and Brent did.

"Septimus?" the Maker asked. "Do you want a second power, knowing the responsibilities it brings?"

"Yes," he replied firmly.

"Brent?"

"Yes," came Brent's quick reply.

The Banquet Hall was silent as the Maker's eyes landed on Samantha.

"And lastly, Samantha. Are you sure you want a second Gift, knowing that it will cause more fatigue?"

"I'm sure. Yes."

The Maker nodded. "Very well. Receive your Gift."

He flipped the three clasps and slowly opened the Chest. At first, nothing happened. But it didn't take long before a white mist began to filter out, and a glowing light struck Septimus.

"To you, the Gift of Strength."

The light disappeared for a brief moment, and then returned and struck Brent. "To you, the Gift of Strength."

Samantha drew in a breath, knowing that she was next. The light vanished and then returned, striking her in the chest and giving her the Gift of Strength as well. The white mist then retreated back into the Chest as the lid shut by itself. In an explosion of bright light, it disappeared.

There was silence as Samantha stared down at her Vest. There was definitely something different now. It was larger and longer and now slid past her hips, over her buttocks. It had short sleeves and looked more like a cloak than a Vest as it shimmered with white, pulsating light. She looked over to Septimus and Brent, both of whom were admiring their long Vests of Light.

"Again, congratulations. Now, it's time to eat. Everyone put on a Belt and eat well."

Septimus turned toward Samantha. "I had my doubts for awhile whether or not you could handle the tournament, but without you, I wouldn't have a second Gift."

He thrust his hand out, and Samantha shook it firmly. "Thanks," she said, welling up with pride.

"Hey, what about me?" Brent cut in sarcastically.

"You, too." Septimus smiled, shaking his hand as well.

"Do you want to come over and eat with my friends?" Samantha asked, motioning toward the table where Juan and George were sitting.

"Thanks, but I'll join the Maker for now," Septimus replied.

"Brent?" Samantha offered.

"Thanks, but I'm eating with Rachel."

The sound of conversation filled the hall as Samantha made her way to the table where George, Juan, Ethan, Jazmin, and Evenina sat. As she passed by other tables, she was congratulated by just about everyone, but it was Pete Harris' comment that made her want to explode with joy.

"I just wanted to say," he said, standing up and stepping in front of her, "that you played terrific."

Samantha felt her cheeks go red.

"And that move you made at the end . . . that was the best," he said, rubbing his hands on his thighs.

"Thanks." Samantha smiled, feeling her face turn hot.

"Hey, Manthers," Juan called from two tables away, "get over here."

Samantha shot Juan an I-don't-want-to-come-over-there look, but he winked at her and said a little louder: "We want to talk to you."

"I'm gonna go sit . . ." Samantha said reluctantly.

"Sure," Pete said shyly, still rubbing his thighs. "Talk to you soon?"

"Okay."

He sat back down while Samantha made her way over to Juan's table.

"You didn't have to do that," she said, taking a seat between Juan and George.

"Do what?"

"Don't start, Juan. I have the Vest of Knowledge and know exactly what you were doing."

Juan looked at her innocently. "What?"

"Never mind," she sighed.

"Samantha, that was such a great move you made at the end," Jazmin said admiringly. "How'd you do it?"

"I really don't know," Samantha admitted, clasping a glowing Belt around her waist, then grabbing a plate and mug. "It just happened . To be honest, it was all luck. I wasn't really trying to get their flag, it just happened to be in the way, and I was lucky enough to grab it.

"Hamburger with everything — fries with ketchup on top and a root beer with ice."

Samantha's food appeared instantaneously.

"Are you fatigued right now?" George asked, staring at Samantha in awe.

"George, you can't get fatigued in the Lighthouse, remember?"

"Oh, yeah."

"So the Gift of Strength, like the guy we met in the barn," Juan joined in. "Do you feel stronger?"

"No," Samantha mumbled before taking a bite of her burger. She was starved.

"C'mon now," Juan said excitedly, sticking out his hand.

"Squeeze it. Squeeze my hand."

Samantha shook her head.

"Samantha — show me how strong you are."

"No," Samantha replied angrily after swallowing.

"What's wrong? Afraid that I . . ."

Samantha didn't let Juan finish. She put her hand into his and felt him grip it firmly. He began to squeeze but not near as strongly as Samantha. She gripped his hand tightly and began to smash his fingers together. His grip was loosening, and it was obvious this was paining him because his face became contorted and misshaped.

"Okay . . . okay," Juan squealed.

Samantha let go and grinned mischievously.

"Dang," Juan said, rubbing his crushed hand with the other. "You *are* strong."

"Well, yeah — you heard the voice," George said sarcastically. "To you, the Gift of Strength. What'd you think, she'd be weak?"

"I wasn't sure how strong she'd really be."

"Well, now you are," George said, returning to his plate of sausage pizza.

"What do you think they're talking about?" Evenina said, pointing to the front table where the Maker, Septimus, Lance, and Nathaniel sat together eating.

"Don't know," said Jazmin between bites. "Can you tell what they're talking about, Samantha?"

"No."

"You know that's the first time I think I've ever seen those four eat together. They're the only adult Brilliants we have, but I hardly ever see them together in the Banquet Hall," said Evenina.

"True," Jazmin acknowledged. "This is the first time we've had this many people together in the hall. It feels good to see everyone together again."

"You know," Evenina said, "we should go to the Garden of Light after we eat. They've never been there."

"Yeah. They'd love it," Jazmin agreed. "But I have to help Alexia in the Library this afternoon until about five. Why don't we go then?"

"The Garden of Light? Where the Weavers and stuff are?" Ethan asked as he took a swig of Pepsi from his mug.

"Right," Evenina replied.

"And maybe tomorrow I can talk Lance into coming with us to Glorrian," Jazmin added.

"What's that?" Juan asked. He'd never heard of Glorrian before and neither had Samantha, Ethan, or George.

"It's a very remote, tropical island. It's really small, no one lives on it, and it's so beautiful. There's a big waterfall we swim in."

"I like waterfalls." Ethan smiled as he remembered Union Creek. "I'll go with you."

"So will I," George said.

"I'm in," added Juan enthusiastically.

Samantha smiled. "So am I."

"Let's meet at nine here in the Banquet Hall. We'll have breakfast, and then we'll go. I'm gonna go ask if Lance wants to come. He's fun to take with us because of his Gift. Be right back," Jazmin said, hopping up from her seat and making her way over to the Maker's table.

"I'm excited about the Garden of Light," Ethan said, finishing his last bite of peanut butter and jelly sandwich. "I'd like to see one of the Weavers."

* * *

Only one Eternal Flame lit the dark, domed cavern, and it burned light blue, casting a strange glow on the few objects that were present: a round glass table, four chairs, and a giant five-foot view screen embedded into one of the rock walls.

"You called for me, sir?" Melt said, stepping into the room.

Xylo looked up and grinned. "It is time to prepare for the bridge."

Melt nodded seriously. "Yes, sir."

"I will attempt the link tonight," Xylo said, narrowing his eyes.

"Very good, sir."

Xylo stood up from the table and moved around it until he was facing Melt. "How long I have waited for this. Finally — finally, we have what we need to defeat the Brilliants. We have a Musicular."

"Yes, we do, sir."

"The bridge will take much out of me, Melt. Fingust is organizing everyone I have requested. I will only be able to send ten of us. You are the team leader. I want you and the others to destroy everything. Take no Brilliants prisoner except for Samantha and the Mathias boy."

Melt nodded.

"As for the Weavers and the Laxinti, I want them captured as well. You are to speak to Malavax. She knows what is needed for the Laxinti. As for the Weavers, your Pulsers should do the job. Lastly, you must get the Book of Light from the Library. Everything else . . . the Garden, the Colossals, everything . . . destroy it all!"

* * *

"Thanks for your help, Jaz," Alexia said as the two girls walked to the center of the Lighthouse. "Couldn't have done it without you."

"No problem," Jazmin smiled. "Are you sure you don't need

anymore help?"

Alexia shook her head. "No, I should be able to finish every-thing up. Aren't you going to the Garden now?"

"Yeah. You wanna come?" Jazmin offered.

"No, but thanks. I want to complete the work here."

Jazmin laughed. "You spend way too much time up in this Library, Alexia."

"You aren't the first person to say that."

Jazmin turned and pushed off into the center. She descend-ed toward the Fountain of Light where her friends stood wait-ing.

"Okay, is everyone here?" Evenina did a head count. "Ethan, Samantha, George, Juan, Jaz . . ."

"Where is Jazmin?" asked George.

"Right here," Jazmin replied, landing behind him. "Just fin-ished up with the Library."

"What were you doing up there, anyway?" Evenina asked.

"Top secret." Jazmin grinned mysteriously.

"Uh-huh," grunted Evenina.

"So, where is this Garden?" Ethan asked as they stood around the splashing Fountain.

"Come on," Evenina said, leading the group toward the enormous doors. As they approached, the left one swung slow-ly open from the push of one of the Colossals.

"As many times as I see those guys, I still can't get over how huge they are," George marveled as they made their way out into the carpet of light.

"Yeah," Juan grunted. "Wouldn't want to make them mad at me."

"The Garden is over in that direction." Jazmin pointed to-ward the moon that looked so close it seemed they could've touched it.

"The Garden's on the moon?" asked Ethan flabbergasted.

"No. You can't see the Garden from here, but as you continue on, it will come into view," Jazmin reassured them as she took the lead.

"What does your Vest tell you about the Garden, Manthers?" asked George as they all walked together.

Samantha concentrated. "It was once on earth, but the Robe moved it here after the Maker completed the Lighthouse."

"The Robe? The guy who saved you that day in the barn?" Ethan asked.

"Our leader," said Evenina reverently. "Even though we have never seen him."

"The Garden is where the seven Weavers live."

"Why did the Robe move it?"

"Too many people and too much interference. There is great power in the Garden, and the Robe didn't want it to be discovered," Samantha said, continuing to follow Jazmin.

"Seven Weavers? And they're the ones who create the Vests?"

"Right, Ethan. They make the Vests out of light. They weave light."

"Fascinating," Ethan whispered.

"There it is," Jazmin said, pointing ahead.

A football field away, the golden carpet of light gave way to the edge of the Garden, a place of such beauty it was breathtaking to behold. As they walked closer, it became clear why it was called the Garden of Light. Everything they saw glowed with an array of color — reds, blues, greens — everything was made of light itself.   "Look at this plant," Juan said, lifting the drooping, trumpet-shaped flower that glistened deep red and yellow.

"What is this place?" George asked as they walked further into the lush vegetation. "I have never seen color like this."

"We won't be able to stay here for very long, maybe a few hours, if we're lucky," Evenina said, stopping to examine a three-foot-tall mushroom pulsating with the colors of the rainbow.

"Why not?" asked Ethan, stopping next to her and staring at the magnificent specimen.

"I don't know. It's like your mind can't take it after awhile, and you have to get out. Maybe you know, Samantha. Why do we get that feeling when we've been in the Garden for a long time?" Evenina wondered.

Samantha shrugged. "Sorry, I'm not getting anything."

"That's all right," Evenina said. "I'm just happy we get to spend time here."

"I've had some wild dreams but nothing like this," Juan said, bending down to look at a bright red tulip just opening. He pulled back in astonishment as it shot out bursts of purple mist.

"The Weavers won't be hard to find," Evenina said, pulling the group to her left and taking the lead. "The Garden isn't that big. When you see them, you're going to have an incredible urge to touch them. I don't know why you get that urge, but everyone does. Whatever you do, don't! They don't like to be touched, and they have the ability to take your Vest right off you." She snapped her fingers. "And you'll lose your power."

"Seriously?" Juan asked with raised eyebrows.

"Yes, even if you don't have your Vest on, they can still take it away. That's what happened to John. Remember that, Jazmin?"

Jazmin nodded.

"Why, what happened?" Ethan wanted to know.

"He touched one of them, and the Weaver stuck out its hand and grabbed John's shoulder and took his Vest away."

"Did he get a new one?"

"No, never did. Lost his Gift."

Evenina led them through a field of deep, knee-high grass rich in colors of green and yellow. She hadn't walked more than twenty feet when to her right she saw the brilliant glowing light.

"There!" She pointed. "There's one!"

Sitting on the ground, partly hidden by enormous blades of grass, was a woman whose hair fell beautifully over her thin body. She was wearing a simple robe that glowed with white light, and in her hands was a mass of what looked like yarn. As Evenina led them all closer, everyone soon realized the mass was light.

"They can control and manipulate light," Jazmin whispered. "You see — she's got some of the Vest already done. Look."

"Yeah, it's partially finished. She's working on the bottom of it. Amazing," Juan whispered excitedly.

"I wonder what power it will have," Ethan spoke quietly.

"We have no way of knowing. Only they know," Jazmin answered in a hush.

"You're right about wanting to touch her," said George longingly. "I feel like going over and hugging her and touching her hair . . . and . . ."

"George, control your emotions," Jazmin snapped.

George shook his head from side to side. "Why do I feel like this?"

"Because love is coming from her. These are Spirits made of light, made completely of love. That's what draws you to them. You want that pure love. That's how powerful love can be," Evenina said, entranced.

"Does she know we're here?"

"Yes," Jazmin said, "but she won't acknowledge us. They never do."

They stared at the maiden as she wove the light slowly and methodically into the Vest. Then to everyone's surprise, the Weaver looked up and fixed her gaze upon them. Her eyes glistened and sparkled with yellows and blues. Everyone stood transfixed.

The Spirit rose, leaving the half-finished Vest on the soft grass, and stepped toward them. She opened her mouth and looked as though she were speaking but no words were coming out. None of them could hear anything except Samantha; she could hear the Weaver perfectly.

"Hello, Samantha Banks. It was I that made your Vest, the Vest of Knowledge." Samantha heard an eloquent voice inside her mind. "You have used your Vest wisely. Many things are expected of you, for the more you know, the more is expected. You will face many challenges and tribulations. Keep your faith and know the Gifts given to you are powerful. Use them and wield them accordingly."

Samantha couldn't speak. She wanted to say something, but she felt frozen, as if she had been ce-mented to the very spot on which she stood. The Weaver smiled so beautifully it was taking all of Juan's power not to rush forward and hold her, to grab her and get a piece of the love that emanated from her.

"Never forget what has been given to you. In your darkest hours, he will come to your aid. Remember his arrows — for they were made here and possess great power. When you most need him, you must call upon him."

* * *

"Those whom you have requested are ready, sir," Melt said, entering the dimly lit room.

"And you've explained everything thoroughly?" Xylo asked, his back to Melt as he stared at the Liqwall.

"Sir, I believe so."

"I trust in no one, not even you, Melt." Xylo turned from the wall and stared coldly. "And I myself would lead the charge if I could, but alas, it falls into your hands. You know what you must do, and I don't care how many Dark Vests die. I want that Book of Light, and you will get if for me, Melt. You'll make sure that they succeed."

"Yes, sir."

"For if they don't," Xylo whispered, now only a few feet away, "I will destroy you first."

Melt had little doubt of this. He had been with his master too long and knew that this mission could easily be his last. But it was a challenge he welcomed, a challenge he longed for.

"I will not fail you, master."

"I hope, for your sake, you're right. Now go and prepare the room."

* * *

"And you heard the Weaver say all those things?" Jazmin asked in amazement as they all sat around the glowing table.

"Yes, I already told you that," Samantha said, before taking a bite of her macaroni and cheese.

"I still can't believe it," Jazmin said, shaking her head.

Evenina finished her bite of lasagna before asking, "What do you think it means that you can understand the Weavers?"

"I don't know," Samantha answered. "I've tried to use my Vest since we've been back, but I'm not getting anything."

"What about when it said that thing about the guy coming to your aid, or whatever," Ethan mentioned seriously.

"Yeah, how are you going to call on him?" Juan asked as he finished a bite of apple.

"I don't know." Samantha shook her head. "But I think I need to begin reading the Book of Light, even though my last experience wasn't the most enjoyable. I need to find out more. I need to understand what's going on."

"It's too bad we didn't see more Weavers," Ethan said.

Evenina smiled. "We should visit again soon."

"Tomorrow, after we get back from Glorrian," Jazmin suggested. "Don't forget, we're leaving in the morning. You're gonna love it there, and Lance is coming with us. That's gonna be fun."

"There is so much to this world," Ethan said. "How long has all of this been around — all the Brilliants and the Dark Vests? Has all of this been around since the beginning of time?"

Everyone turned to Samantha for the answer.

"My Vest tells me the answer lies in the Book of Light. In it is the history of the Brilliants and the Dark Vests. I need to learn what that history is."

"Excuse me," came Pete's voice behind Samantha.

"Hi, Pete," Samantha said, turning her head.

"Hi, Sam. I was wondering if you might want to go for a walk?"

Samantha looked at Jazmin and smiled, then back to Pete. "Yeah, that'd be great."

"You don't need to if you're not done," said Pete.

"It's okay. I'm finished. Clean up."

Samantha's dishes disappeared as she turned and walked with Pete out of the Banquet Hall.

"It's pretty obvious the two of them like each other. Did you see the way he looked at her?" expressed Ethan.

"Juan? What's wrong with you?" Evenina asked, having noticed Juan's nasty glare as Pete and Samantha went around the corner and out of sight.

"I don't like him," Juan said darkly.

"Pete's a good guy," Jazmin said smiling. "He's been here for almost a year. A lot of the girls like him."

"You're jealous, aren't you?" Evenina said, leaning over the table toward Juan.

"Shut up. I'm not jealous. It's just that there's something about that guy that bugs me. I don't know what it is, but I could've sworn that when he walked out just a second ago, a streak of black went up his Vest."

"What?" George said, frowning. "Come on, now."

"No, I'm serious. I watched them all the way out and at right about the corner there, I saw a black, sparkling streak. Now, I've seen Dark Vests before, and they all sparkle just like what I saw."

"You are so making that up!" Evenina said. "It's obvious you like Samantha."

"Yeah, I like Samantha . . . like a sister, and usually I'm pretty good at judging how people are. Right, George?"

George nodded. "Juan has this thing about people. He seems to be able to tell what kind of a person they are right from the start."

"I agree with Evenina; I think you're jealous," Jazmin said.

"You want me to take the dude out?" Ethan asked Juan seriously. "I'll smash into him like I did that Dark Vest on the bus."

"You will not!" Jazmin raised her voice. "He's a good person."

"Maybe, and maybe not, Jazmin. But if he hurts one of my best friends, he's in for the wrath of Juan."

Evenina and Jazmin burst out laughing, but Ethan and George looked just as serious as Juan did.

* * *

"This will do nicely," Xylo said approvingly as Melt followed him into the cave-like room lit by an Eternal Flame that burned bright red. "It is imperative that I am not to be disturbed at any time until the bridge is complete. You understand, Melt?"

Melt nodded seriously.

"What does your watch say?"

"Eight o'clock, sir."

"It will take me many hours to make the bridge. I want you to come back and check on me at ten o'clock tomorrow morning. If everything goes as planned, the link will be established, and you'll be able to bridge."

"Yes, sir."

"Now," Xylo said, striding to the small cot in the center of the room, "I will begin the process. Leave me, and do not return until morning."

"Sir."

Xylo climbed onto the cot and lay on his back, shifting around until he was comfortable. He propped the pillow up under his head and shut his eyes, just as Melt closed the sliding, stone door.

★ ★ ★

"About time you showed up," Juan said angrily as Samantha walked into Jazmin and Evenina's quarters.

"What?" Samantha said, walking toward a chair.

"You've been gone all this time with Pete."

"Yeah, so?" Samantha sat down at the table with everyone else and frowned back at Juan. "Is that okay with you, Juan?"

Juan bit his lip and frowned.

"So where did you go?" Jazmin quickly changed the subject.

"We just walked around the Lighthouse," Samantha answered pleasantly. "You know, he's really nice. He talked about ..."

Juan grunted loudly.

Samantha was clearly becoming agitated. "What's your problem, Juan?"

Ethan shot a look over to George. He was sensing the same tension everyone else in the room was.

"All right, I wasn't going to say anything, but ..."

"Don't, Juan!" Evenina said, pointing.

"But she has to hear it! I know what I saw!"

"What? What did you see?" Samantha said angrily.

"Samantha, when you were walking out, I saw a streak of

black, just like the Dark Vests, on Pete's back. It was there for only a second, and then it went away, but I'm telling you, I saw it."

Samantha was breathing heavily with anger. "I don't know why you don't like him, Juan. Maybe you're jealous or whatever, but making stuff up about him is low."

"I am not making stuff up! I saw it!"

"Did anyone else see it, Juan? Did you see it, Ethan?"

Ethan shook his head no.

"What about you, Jazmin? Evenina?"

The two girls shook their heads. Samantha looked at George. "George, did you see it?"

George swallowed hard. It was difficult to see his two best friends in a fight. "No, I didn't, but I think you should listen."

"There you go, Juan. No one else saw it. I was walking with him, and I never saw it."

"I told you it was on his back!"

"Why are you doing this?" Samantha raised her voice higher. "I really like him!"

"I'm just trying to help you. I know what I saw, and I'm a pretty good judge of character, Samantha. You remember Chelsea from Bennett? You remember when I told you that I knew she was just faking about being your friend? And what about last year with Susan? I was right about both of them."

"But Pete's nice. He listens, and I know he cares for me."

"Manthers, I've known you for a long time, and I'm not jealous. I'm concerned."

"Well, don't be, Dad," Samantha laughed sarcastically. "Juan, why don't you just mind your own business!"

Juan turned to look at George for support. George shook his head.

"Why don't you guys leave!"

Juan stood up and slid his chair back to the table quietly. "Just be careful, Manthers. I'm telling you, and everyone here has heard it. Pete is evil. And I'm gonna say this, and it's gonna make you mad, but I think he's a Dark Vest."

"What!" erupted Samantha.

"Juan, that's enough!" Jazmin shouted.

"Think about it!" Juan shouted back. "He has the Gift of Color! He could change his Vest's color!"

"No, he can't! He told me that's the one thing he can't change!" Samantha retorted.

"Or at least he says he can't change it. If he was a Dark Vest, do you think he'd tell ya?"

This was the final straw. Samantha burst into tears, and Evenina and Jazmin were quickly at her side, comforting her and shooting looks of venom at Juan.

"Come on," George said, pulling Juan by the arm. "Let's go."

"Manthers, I'm sorry, but I just had to."

"Get out!" Samantha shouted.

"Let's go, Juan," Ethan said.

"I'm telling you, he's a Dark Vest. He's evil," Juan said as George and Ethan escorted him out of the room.

Samantha spent the next hour talking with Evenina and Jazmin about Pete, and when she was finished, there was little doubt in her mind that he was one of the nicest guys in the Lighthouse, and that Juan was fanatically jealous.

By the time Samantha slid into bed, she felt ex-hausted, both physically, for it had been a physically challenging day, and mentally, because of the stress Juan had added. It took only a minute before she was sound asleep.

For a while she slept soundly, as the pool of drool on her pillow proved, but around one-thirty, she heard a voice calling her in the distance. It grew steadily louder, calling her again and again.

"Samantha, come. Come and play me," the voice spoke quietly. "I want you to come and play me."

Samantha opened her eyes slowly as the voice continued.

"Come here . . . Come here . . ."

Part of her wanted to stay in bed and finish the slumber she had just started to enjoy, but a larger part of her wanted to follow the voice and do as it said. She had a longing — a desire to please it.

"Come to the Music Room, and I will show you."

Samantha got out of bed, staring blankly, following the orders of the voice as though she were hypnotized. She stayed in her light-blue and yellow pajamas, and it took her only a couple of minutes to float past the splashing Fountain of Light and glide smoothly up until she was once again in the Music Room.

"Come and pick up my mallets, and I will show you . . ." the voice summoned.

She stepped around a floating French horn and then past a sparkling clarinet as she made her way to the xylophone that shimmered like gold.

"Samantha, what are you doing?" Cfage, the grand piano, said, pounding out a set of choppy chords.

Samantha wanted to respond, but something inside her wasn't letting her talk.

"Ignore all that you hear. Obey my voice only. Come to me, now."

She was drawing closer but now it wasn't just Cfage trying to stop her. Nearly all the instruments were beginning to pound out notes, and every message was the same: Don't listen to the voice. Don't touch the xylophone.

But Samantha couldn't resist. She was controlled by an unknown force, and her desire to play had overtaken her. She stood in front of the xylophone.

"Pick up the mallets."

Again, the other instruments burst out in objection, but it was useless. She reached down and picked up the mallets, one in each hand.

"Play me! PLAY ME!"

Then she did what all the instruments had warned her not to do. As soon as she touched the bars of the xylophone, she felt her desire increase. She wanted to play and play. This desire was filling her with a feeling she had never experienced, a feeling of power, lust, of belonging.

"Very good. Keep playing me. Feel my power within you. Answer my questions."

She couldn't hear the rest of the instruments blaring out their warnings anymore. All she could hear was the voice as it beckoned her to continue playing. And play she did.

DESTRUCTION
September 20

"About time," George said as the doors slid apart quickly. "I've been pounding on the door for half an hour."

Samantha wiped the sleep from her eyes and gestured her friend into the room.

"I was wondering . . . whoa, you look like you had a long night. Didn't you get enough sleep?"

"I . . . I . . . ," Samantha stammered. "I don't think I slept well."

"Yeah, that's obvious," George said flatly.

"I had a strange dream. At least, I think it was a dream," Samantha muttered slowly.

George frowned. "What are you talking about?"

"Did you ever have a dream that seemed real? I mean, as if it all really happened? Have you ever dreamed like that?"

"Yeah, once in awhile," George admitted.

Samantha turned away and stared blankly out the window that overlooked earth.

"Manthers . . . hello? What was the dream about?"

"Oh, nothing. It . . . was . . . nothing."

"Doesn't seem like nothing," George said, stepping forward and taking a closer look at her. "Do you still want to come with us to Glorrian?"

"What?"

"Glorrian? You know, the island."

"Oh, yes." Samantha brushed her hands through her tangled hair that reminded George of a scrambled mess of fishing line.

"You all right?"

"Fine," Samantha sighed. "Yes, okay. Glorrian. I'll go to Glorrian."

"You must be tired 'cause you're acting weird."

"What time is it now?"

"Almost nine. We're having breakfast in a few minutes, and then we're leaving right after that because Lance has to get back by noon. This was the only time he could go."

"Okay, let me get changed really quick, and I'll meet you there. Where's Juan?"

"He's still pretty upset about last night. He's up in the Banquet Hall."

"Oh, right," Samantha said, shaking her head as if trying to shake off a headache. "He's still going on about Pete? I hope not."

"He's calmed down. What about you?"

"I'm better," she replied, staring out the window again.

"You sure you're okay?" George asked, still not convinced Samantha was her normal self.

Samantha tried to be brighter, in spite of feeling sluggish and dazed. "I'm fine, George. Go on. I'll see you in a couple of minutes."

A couple of minutes turned about to be forty-five, and by the time Samantha arrived at the Banquet Hall, the others were finishing up their breakfasts. The hall was filled with other Brilliants, many of whom congratulated Samantha as she made her way to her friends' table.

"What took you so long?" George wondered as he stuffed the last bite of waffle into his mouth.

"I stayed in the shower a little too long."

"You look pale. Are you feeling okay?" Jazmin said, noticing the dark circles under Samantha's eyes.

"I'm fine."

"You'd better get some breakfast," Lance suggested, motioning for Samantha to take a chair.

"Orange juice — full."

"That's it? You're not hungry?" asked Evenina.

"No, I don't have much of an appetite."

Juan and George looked at each other. It wasn't like Samantha to not eat. They had known her long enough to realize that she wasn't being herself. She seemed down, not just tired, but almost exhausted. Neither said anything, blaming it on a lack of sleep.

"Hey, Manthers, I'm sorry about what I said last night," Juan said sincerely.

Samantha looked at him kindly, but there was something about her gaze that looked distant and empty. "I'm sorry, too," she whispered.

"Friends?" Juan asked, raising his eyebrows hopefully.

"Always." Samantha smiled weakly.

"You don't have your Vest on today," Evenina observed while Samantha took a swig of juice.

"Oh, guess not," Samantha said, staring down at her chest.

"It's weird to see you without it."

Samantha grinned. She didn't know if this was an invitation for her to don her Vest, but she didn't feel like putting it on so she took another drink instead.

"This is going to be fun!" Evenina shifted gears enthusiastically. "You're going to love Glorrian, and especially if Lance can call the birds."

"The birds?" George looked across the table at Lance.

"A variety of birds live on the island. I call them in, and they put on a kind of aerial show for us. It's really fun to watch," Lance answered eagerly.

"Cool."

When Samantha had finished her orange juice, and the rest of them had scraped the last food from their plates, Jazmin leaned forward, speaking softly. "Now get ready because I'm going to transport us . . ."

"Hey," came Fox's voice as he rolled toward their table. "Have you heard?"

Jazmin turned, irritated by the interruption. "Fox, we were just about to . . ."

"The instruments in the Music Room are going nuts. They're all playing this weird music, and it sounds terrible. A bunch of us were wonderin' if you were gonna go up and see what they're sayin'," he said, looking at Samantha.

Samantha felt something inside her sink, like a rock had been dropped into her stomach. Before she could answer, Evenina interjected.

"We're about to go to Glorrian. Can't it wait? We only have a little time with Lance, and we really want to get there."

"Oh." Fox nodded. "Sorry, I didn't know. Yeah, it can wait. I mean, I don't think it's a big deal or anything — just kinda weird. That's never happened since I've been here."

Samantha wanted more than ever to get up and go to the Music Room so she could listen to what the instruments were saying, but she didn't need her Vest to know that everyone at the table wanted to visit the tropical island rather than go up and listen to a bunch of instruments they couldn't understand.

Fox turned his wheelchair around and began to scoot away. "You might want to take a listen when you get back," he said, making his way to the corridor.

"She will," Evenina answered for her. "Okay, let's go."

"Get ready," Jazmin said, her Vest sparkling with bright light. But before she could transport everyone, Mathias Braxton touched her on the shoulder.

"I heard where you're going," he said pleasantly, "and I want to go. Take me, take me."

"No," she said sternly.

"Please. I like that place."

"No, Mathias."

"Jazmin — please."

"Mathias," came Lance's voice, "we will allow you to come but only if you promise to remain as Mathias and not Braxton while we're there. Can you promise that?"

It was obvious by the looks on everyone's faces at the table that they doubted the boy could actually live up to the promise.

"I promise," he said firmly.

Everyone except Lance looked thoroughly displeased. "Then you may come," said Lance evenly.

"You actually believe him? After all the stuff he's done in the past?"

"If he doesn't come, I don't come," Lance retorted.

Mathias was smiling brightly and staring at Lance thankfully.

"Ah —" Jazmin waved her hand flippantly before picking up a large duffle bag stuffed with towels. "Hope everyone has their swimsuit on underneath their clothes. I'll bet you it's hot in Glorrian."

In a flash of golden light, the table of people along with Mathias disappeared. When they materialized, they were standing at the base of a magnificent waterfall some one hundred and fifty feet high. Water plummeted over the narrow ledge and smashed down into a large, deep blue pool. The sun was intensely hot in the cloudless sky. The hundred degree heat was tolerable only because they were standing so close to nature's air conditioner.

"What a place," George said in wonder.

"Yeah," Juan grunted in agreement.

Samantha was equally impressed by the beauty. As she stared at the falls, a weight seem to lift from her, and for the first time that morning she felt normal and more awake.

"I love this place," said Jazmin, walking to the edge of the pool of water.

"This reminds me of Union Creek," Ethan said, staring around at the massive vegetation. Union Creek Falls was remote but not nearly as remote as this. It was clear that very few humans had ever been where Ethan and his friends were standing.

"I forgot how wonderful it is here," Mathias said in a reflective voice. "It's been a long time."

"Yes, it has," Jazmin agreed. "Well, for you first-timers, welcome to the island of Glorrian and Glorrian Falls — named after Glorrian Gallaps."

"Who was that?" Juan asked, closing his eyes and letting the sun's rays beat down on his face.

Jazmin's eyes shot to the ground, and she was silent for a few moments before saying softly, "Glorrian was a Brilliant who discovered this island and showed it to me a few years ago. We've been coming ever since."

"Where is she now?" Ethan asked carefully, afraid of what the answer might be.

Jazmin sighed deeply before answering. "Glorrian was killed by Xylo."

* * *

Tom Kitts, Pete Harris, Fox Thomas, and Raul Martinez were standing together, staring incredulously as instruments of all sorts rattled, blew, strummed, and banged out some of the most obnoxious sounds any of them had ever heard.

"Man, it's loud," Pete shouted over the noise. "How long is this gonna go on?"

"Don't know," Fox yelled back. "I told Samantha, but she went with Jazmin and the others."

"C'mon, let's go." Tom gestured back to the middle of the Lighthouse. "We're the only ones still up here. Everyone else already left."

"I don't know," Fox said seriously. "There's something weird about all of this."

Pete shrugged dismissively. "Forget about it. I'm outta here."

"We should go tell the Maker or Septimus," Raul offered.

"Go ahead, but I'm going back to my room," Pete shouted over the noise and floated off.

"Hey, look there. What is that?" Fox said, pointing.

"You mean the instrument? That's a xylophone," replied Tom.

"Yeah, but why is it turning black?"

"Whoa, Fox, you're right. Look at that. It's almost completely black now!" Tom said.

"What's that other light next to it? It's getting bigger," Raul observed, pointing.

"It's getting too loud in here. I can barely hear you guys," Tom shouted over the thundering noise.

"What about that light? It's taking the shape of a circle and what's that stuff coming down from it? Looks like syrup," Fox said apprehensively. "We better get the Maker and see what he thinks."

"Wait," Raul shot out, pointing along with Tom. "There's something coming out of it."

"What is that?" Fox asked.

But that was the last word any of them heard before they died, for out of the syrupy black portal emerged the first of ten Dark Vests, and the very first one to appear was Melt.

What the boys saw was a tall, dark-robed, and masked man point his hand toward them. Before they had time to react, the Brilliants dropped to the floor dead, their hearts melted within seconds.

Every Dark Vest who followed was dressed in the same dark robes, and all were wearing black masks hidden under the dark shadows of their hoods. The masks made them look faceless and death-like, which was precisely why Xylo had insisted they wear them. The element of surprise, even for a brief second, was an advantage Melt had already exploited.

The noise within the Music Room was deafening, but it wasn't long until the sound subsided as Melt systematically dissolved each of the instruments until there was silence. "Take out your Pulsers and be ready," he ordered as the last violin melted away.

The other nine Dark Vests reached into their holsters and pulled out what looked like medium-sized horseshoes, equipped with eight-inch handles and triggers. Each weapon looked exactly the same and shimmered with black light.

"Malavax with me. The rest of you know your orders. We don't have a lot of time."

Melt led the charge to the center, followed by Malavax and the rest. He pushed upward as the others descended to the lower floors. Within a few seconds, he was standing in the Library. For a moment, he was distracted by the floating shelves of books.

"Remember who we're looking for. Don't kill anyone unless you know for sure it is not Alexia."

Malavax nodded, holding her weapon up and pointing it in various directions. The two moved through the shelves slowly and were about to turn down a long aisle when a movement to their left caught their attention. Malavax turned to see Jeremy Erikson, a tall, black-haired boy, staring at her in fear. Malavax pressed the trigger and a tennis ball-sized orb of red and black shot out silently and struck Jeremy in the chest. He staggered for a moment, gripped his breast, and then fell to the floor, dead.

"This way," Melt said, whisking Malavax down a different aisle.

A small girl with a brilliant Vest of Light was reading cross-legged on the ground forty feet ahead of them. The girl was too involved in the book to know that enemies were near and felt only a short blast of pain before everything around her turned white and silent.

Malavax and Melt stepped over the girl's limp body and made their way forward without hesitation or remorse. Just as they came to the end of the aisle, they spotted what they were looking for. There was no mistaking the flowing blond hair. It was the librarian, Alexia Pearson, just as Samantha had described her.

Alexia had no idea that her Library was under attack or that two of the vilest people in the world were now standing behind her only a few feet away.

"Librarian," Melt shot out a whisper.

Alexia turned around and stared in horror at the masked robes.

"Don't even scream, for if you do, I'll melt your legs," Melt said savagely, raising his right arm and pointing at her. "Take us to the Book of Light."

Alexia stood, frozen in fear.

"Take us to the Book of Light," Melt repeated, "or everyone in this place will die, including you."

Alexia's breathing was choked and spotty as she tried to regain her composure.

"I . . . will . . . not . . ." she said as strongly as possible.

A black light exploded from Melt's hand as Alexia's right thumb dissolved away. She shrieked in terror and grabbed it with her other hand, trying to stop the blood.

"Take us to the Book!" Melt screamed. "THE BOOK!"

Alexia made an attempt to lunge at Melt, but he backed away quickly.

"Nice try, Brilliant. I don't want any part of your Gift. Now, the Book!"

"I . . . will . . . not!"

Another blast of black, and her other thumb was gone.

"The next thing I melt won't be on your hand. Unless you're willing to die along with everyone else in this place, you'll take me to the Book. This is your last warning. Take us now or be melted to nothing!"

Alexia bit her lower lip to hold back the tears. There was no mistaking that she was in pain. Her thumbs were now bloody stubs, and she had no choice but to lead the two Dark Vests reluctantly toward their prize. As she led them down a long aisle of books, Copalis Morgan, a boy of sixteen with red hair, stood leaning against one of the golden pillars, engrossed in a book.

Before she could warn him, he fell to the ground in a dead heap. She wheeled around, tears rolling down her cheeks.

"No! No! Why?"

"Until I have the Book, everyone I see dies!"

"He . . . curse you!" Alexia screamed.

"THE BOOK!"

Alexia walked slowly past Copalis' lifeless body and around the pillar to another aisle. The Library was silent, a terrible silent. She was hoping someone would see her, that someone would see the Dark Vests . . . the Maker, Septimus, anyone . . . but there was no one. Three aisles later, she was standing in front of the door that led to the Book of Light.

"This is it?" Melt asked, standing a good distance behind Alexia and behind him, Malavax.

Alexia nodded solemnly. "I shouldn't have showed you," she whispered.

Melt smiled wickedly.

"You're going to kill me anyway," Alexia said, tears falling randomly down her cheeks.

Melt raised both hands and two beams of black light hit the door. It wasn't three seconds before it was disintegrated, exposing the pulsating Book of Light resting on a tall bookstand.

"I will not need you now," Melt laughed, and that was the last thing Alexia heard before she fell to the floor.

Melt walked forward and grabbed the Book. He held it a moment, then passed it to Malavax. "Let's move."

They sprinted back through the maze of aisles and floating shelves toward the middle of the Lighthouse.

"Get back to the portal and get out of here. Go now!" Melt ordered.

Malavax floated above him, heading back to the Music Room as Melt dove down to the fourth floor. He landed and almost melted Fury, who surprised him.

"We've killed eight so far," Fury said proudly, out of breath.

Melt nodded his head approvingly. "Get the rest of your company and meet us on the first floor."

"Yes, sir," Fury said, rushing away.

★ ★ ★

Septimus didn't recognize the voice he heard coming down the corridor. It was a deep, adult voice, and it did not belong to anyone he knew.

"You take the left. I have the right," the voice ordered.

Septimus took a breath and stayed at the corner, his back against the glowing wall. There were two of them. Were they new Brilliants? No, impossible. The voice he heard was unfamiliar to him, and that could only mean one thing: The Dark Vests, as impossible as it seemed, had discovered a way into the Lighthouse. But how? That was a question he couldn't worry about at the moment.

He stepped forward and slid his head out around the corner. The long hallway was filled with doors to the left and the right, all training rooms, and he barely caught a glimpse of two men entering two of the rooms. Septimus felt his pulse quicken, and he clinched his sweaty fists hard as a Vest of Light wrapped around his upper body.

He would start with the door to his left. He pulled the Vest-shaped handle and stepped into the room quietly, readying himself. Across the large tiled room, a robed figure was bent over a computer-like screen embedded into one of the golden desks that lined the wall, his back to Septimus.

"Hailey, come look at this," the man said, a Dark Vest shimmering across his back. He had obviously heard the door open behind him. "I think it's a map of the entire Lighthouse."

Septimus walked methodically over, his apprehension being quickly replaced with rage.

"Yeah, this is a map. It shows everything! Wait   until . . ." the man said enthusiastically, turning around.

"Cute mask," Septimus said, his eyes narrowed in fury.

"Time to die, Brilliant," the Dark Vest shouted with a warped sense of glory, shoving both arms forward.

Septimus didn't know who this man was or what power he had, but it really didn't matter. He didn't need to know in order for his Gift of Defense to be effective.

The Dark Vest shoved his arms forward again, as if to jump-start his power.

No power.

"What the . . ."

"Your Gift doesn't work!" And with that, Septimus took two quick steps forward and landed a fist in the man's stomach, bending him over. "To you, the Gift of Defense — the ability to stop another's Gift."

The enemy coughed violently.

"You won't be needing that mask," Septimus said darkly and gave the Dark Vest an uppercut with his foot. There was a loud popping noise as the man's jaw broke, and the mask tumbled off his face as he fell backwards to the ground.

Septimus bent down and picked the mask up, staring at the faceless disguise. He then looked over at the enemy, bleeding from the mouth and staggering to get up.

Septimus stared at him and crushed the mask into pieces. The Dark Vest stared wild-eyed. He attempted to bring his watch up to his mouth, but Septimus reached out and snapped his wrist like it was a pencil. The pain sent the enemy to his knees.

"How did you get in?" Septimus stood over him, still holding his limp wrist.

The Dark Vest mumbled something, but it was incoherent. His jaw was broken in three places.

"How many Vests are here? Tell me! Use your fingers with your good hand."

The enemy grimaced in pain.

"Show me!"

The enemy showed five fingers, followed by a fist, then five fingers again.

"Ten?"

The enemy nodded.

Septimus let go of the man's wrist and with one forward kick, ended his life. He turned, his rage boiling. There was another Dark Vest directly across in the next room. He moved forward and reached for the handle but paused as the door began to open. He stepped back and waited until the enemy was in full view. With a quick left hand, he tore the enemy's mask off and at the same time, reared back with his right, punching the enemy squarely in the face. Blood exploded everywhere as the blow broke her nose and sent her reeling backwards into the hallway. The hood of her robe fell from her head, exposing her jet-black hair.

"Please, please," the woman wailed from the ground. "Oh, please."

Septimus crushed the mask into pieces just like he had the last one.

"You're Septimus — Septimus Flynn. Oh . . ."

"How did you get in?" Septimus barked. The fact that this enemy was a woman had no bearing on him. She would've killed him had her power not been rendered useless.

"We . . . we . . ."

"How?"

"The Music Room," came her answer in a whisper.

"The music . . ."

The woman was getting to her feet, blood running profusely from her nose. "Please, don't kill me. I was just following orders."

"Whose orders?"

The woman backed up slowly, her right arm disappearing behind her back.

Did she think he didn't notice? Did she think he was that slow?

"Whose orders?" Septimus shouted.

The woman had found what she was searching for and pulled it out, pointing it at Septimus with sudden vigor. "Xylo's orders," she said wickedly, her tone quite different now that she was holding a Pulser in her hand.

"Xylo's and not Melt's?" Septimus said, undeterred by the weapon.

"I know your power," the woman hissed. "It only works on Vests, which means that this Pulser is all I need to kill you."

Septimus smiled.

This took the enemy aback. She frowned. How could he be smiling when she had the upper hand?

"Was it Xylo or Melt that gave the order?"

"Yes, you would want to know that, wouldn't you? Since it was Melt who killed your family. Now it will be I who kill you. Melt will be pleased."

"Are you sure?" Septimus' smile broadened.

"Oh, most definitely."

"About killing me? How can you do that when you're about

to be eaten?"

The enemy's eyes flashed to her side.

"What are you talking about?"

"Behind you."

"Oh, please, as if I would take your bait. Time to die, Septimus." She aimed the Pulser at his head. But from behind her came a growl so loud it shook the ground, and the force of the giant dog's breath swept the woman's robe high into the air. Before she could turn around and see the beast, it had chomped down. The Pulser fell out of her hand as the dog lifted her into the air, tossing her down the hallway.

Septimus turned and walked toward the woman as the dog followed, so large it had to squeeze its way forward in between the walls.

"You said the Music Room. How did you use the Music Room to get in?"

The enemy was holding her stomach in intense pain.

"The Music Room!" Septimus shouted.

"The xylophone!" the woman shouted back. "Xylo made a bridge with the xylophone."

Septimus stared at her for a few moments then turned toward the dog. "Eat her," he said, and ducked as the giant golden dog squeezed its way over him and in one screaming bite, swallowed the Dark Vest whole.

"Thanks, I owe you," Septimus said, walking toward the Maker who was staring at the dog he had made.

"Luckily, I saw you in time. I fear there are more dark Vests here."

"Ten . . . well, now eight."

"We must protect the others. Dog . . . dissolve."

The giant creature disappeared as the two men ran toward the center of the Lighthouse.

"I'll go to the Music Room and see what I can find out about the xylophone," Septimus said, approaching the center.

The Maker was about to tell Septimus he was going to check the other floors but couldn't because he was struck in the chest with a blast of black light. He fell to his knees, gripping his chest.

"NO!" Septimus screamed.

Another blast collided with the Maker's head, and his body was propelled backwards violently. Septimus looked above him and saw the enemy floating, Pulser aimed. Septimus leapt into the middle and gave a quick jerk to his left as he ascended. The Dark Vest fired but missed right. He fired again and missed high. He wouldn't get a chance to fire again. Septimus was upon him and grabbed the weapon, at the same time kicking the man in the chest. The blow sent him out the middle and up to the next floor.

Breathing heavily and suddenly weighed down by grief, Septimus floated back to the Maker, whose body lay motionless on the glowing floor. He bent over and checked his pulse. However faint, his friend had a heartbeat. He slid his arm underneath the Maker's head and picked him up, when a blast of dark light hit the benevolent leader in the neck, knocking both men backwards. Septimus scrambled to his feet, but soon realized that the Pulser he'd been holding was ten feet to his left. Standing in front of him were three Dark Vests, and the middle one was removing his mask.

"MELT!" Septimus said savagely.

"Septimus . . . my dear friend, Septimus." Melt raised his Pulser and fired two more shots into the Maker's now lifeless body.

"MELT!" Septimus spat, watching the Maker's limp frame bounce across the floor.

Septimus was rage itself, his Vest pulsating brightly with wild, bright light. Melt raised his weapon. "Too bad your Gift doesn't work on weapons. I find it fitting that I finish what I began so long ago."

Septimus' eyes went from Melt to the hooded enemy on his right, then on his left, each pointing a Pulser as well.

"Your family . . . the Maker . . . and now, you."

However futile, Septimus charged with everything he had. It wasn't enough. The pain he felt in his chest was sharp and quick before everything went white. Melt walked over and stood over Septimus' dead body, looked at it for a few seconds, then spit on it.

★ ★ ★

The water was refreshing, and everyone, except for Mathias and Lance, were indulging themselves in the deep pool at the base of Glorrian Falls. George popped his head through the surface and looked for Juan. "Where'd you go?" he shouted. "You better not have turned invisible!"

"Remember the rule," Samantha said, breaststroking toward the bank. "You can't use your Vest."

"Yeah, but I can't find him," complained George, looking around the pool feverishly.

Juan's head finally surfaced near the falls. "C'mon George — you're it. Come get me."

"Don't worry, I'm comin'."

But George was really trying to distract Jazmin who was closest to him. He dove down into the water, pushed off the sandy bottom, and shot in her direction. He could see her blurred legs underwater as he kicked toward her.

Jazmin dove to her left and kicked madly, but George was already too close and touched her ankle.

"Jazmin's it," he shouted as he surfaced.

"Ah!" Jazmin said, spitting out a mouthful of water. "Lucky."

"Hey, wait — look," Evenina said from the other side of the pool. "Up there."

Everyone stared above. Flying around in whirling circles were small birds of every color, darting back and forth, up and down. Samantha moved her eyes to the bank and saw Lance's Vest shining brilliantly as his attention was fixed upon the birds.

"He's talking to them," Evenina said to Samantha who was close by in the water. "He gets them to put on this aerial display. It's fantastic!"

Samantha watched, astonished as more birds joined in until wings of every sort filled the sky above them. Birds rested on Lance's shoulders, as if he were a tree, and nibbled on his ears affectionately.

"It's incredible," Samantha marveled. "Look at them all."

A small, red-yellow bird skimmed the top of her ear.

She laughed.

"What kind of birds are these?" Ethan asked, directing his question to Lance.

Lance shrugged. "Don't know," he answered as a bright blue bird landed on top of his head. "Get off," he scolded. "Go on. Get off."

The bird flew off reluctantly and settled for a crowded shoulder. "Why don't you use your Vest, Samantha, and find out what kind of birds they are," Lance suggested as more birds dazzled the audience with fancy aerial moves.

"With pleasure," Samantha called, and immediately her long Vest of Light appeared.

She was ready to ask about the birds when a heavy feeling came over her like a thick blanket. It was the same feeling she had felt earlier in the day at the Lighthouse, a fatigue unlike any she had ever experienced before.

It was obvious something had come over her because Evenina asked, "Are you all right? You look sick all of a sudden."

Samantha coughed. "I don't know." Then the pain hit her like a baseball bat to the stomach; a throbbing, burning pain seemed to be erupting in her insides.

"Ah!" she screamed, holding her stomach.

"What is it? What's wrong?" Evenina said, worried.

"Help me to the bank," Samantha said, reaching out for Evenina's arm.

Evenina made her way through the wavy, three-foot deep water, grabbing Samantha's hand firmly and helping her to the bank.

"What's going on? What's wrong?" George swam over, followed by Ethan and Juan.

"I don't know," Evenina said as Samantha fell onto the sand, holding her stomach.

"The pain," she grunted.

It wasn't long before Lance, Mathias, and Jazmin were standing over Samantha as well.

"Where's it hurt?" Lance asked while birds continued to buzz overhead.

"Stomach," Samantha managed. "But there's something else. Something's wrong . . . something's wrong at the Lighthouse."

"The Lighthouse?" Lance frowned.

"What's wrong at the Lighthouse?" Jazmin asked, bending over and taking Samantha's hand.

"Something terrible has happened there," Samantha replied, now almost in a whisper.

"The Lighthouse? Nothing bad can happen there, Samantha."

"No," Samantha said, shaking her head. "No, you're wrong, Evenina. Something very evil has happened there. We have to go back. We have to go back now!"

Everyone turned and looked at Lance. He was the adult. He was the most experienced. He would know what to do.

"Jazmin, do as she says. Take us back —"

In a brilliant flash of light, the eight of them disappeared, not knowing what to expect . . . not knowing that only vicious evil awaited them.

LET THE BATTLE CONCLUDE
IN THE *THREE VESTS III: HEROES*

"You didn't think you'd get out of the Triangle alive, did you?"

www.threevests.com

Breinigsville, PA USA
22 February 2010
232944BV00001B/2/P